Matters
TO YOU

The Hart Series
book five

M.E. CARTER

Matters

TO YOU

The Hart Series
book five

ONE

Kiersten

"**I**'m so sorry it's taking me longer than expected, babe. I promise I'll be there as soon as I can."

I smile into the phone as my boyfriend and father of my unborn child does his best to beg forgiveness for not being home in time to help me register for all things baby.

"If I didn't know better, I'd say you planned it this way so you could get out of it."

He scoffs and then laughs, likely seeing the same irony I do—he's been complaining about having to do this for a week and once he's finally on board, the weather is what thwarts our plans.

I can't stay mad at him for it, though. Spencer Woodrow and I had only been dating for a couple of months when we found out I was pregnant. Having a baby at twenty-one years old wasn't in either of our plans and took some adjusting for both of us. But I have to admit, six months into the pregnancy and it hasn't been horrible so far. I have a loving, supportive boyfriend. I have loving, supportive friends. And I'm one of those obnoxious women who feels fantastic during pregnancy—all glowy and cute and healthy.

The only downside is my parents have all but disowned me, not that I'm surprised. The perfection of Kiersten Willoughby, or more accurately lack thereof, has always been a point of contention in our relationship. Probably because I gave up trying long ago and started doing my own thing. That meant ditching pointe shoes and pink leotards for dancing heels and booty shorts. No, I'm not a stripper. Contemporary dance is just more my style. Ballet doesn't give me the same type of creativity. Not to mention, jobs are much harder to come by.

Not that I'll be working in my profession of choice any time soon. My huge baby bump put a temporary hold on that pretty damn quick. It's remarkable how even the most liberal-minded parent suddenly thinks twice when they learn their child's dance teacher is an unmarried pregnant college student. Or at least that was the explanation my boss gave me when I was "relieved of my duties." Who knows? Maybe it was actually her disdain for seeing a baby bump in a leotard. Regardless, it's a right-to-work state, and fighting it under the legal guise of "discrimination" was too much effort.

Besides, Spence comes from a well-to-do family. It's not like his baby will want for anything. He assures me all the time as soon as his parents meet me and more importantly, our son, they'll fall in love with both of us.

"While I appreciate that I get to miss part of our appointment, I can't take credit for my absence," Spence jokes. "My study group ran long and now it's raining really hard. Are you sure you don't want to reschedule?"

"You know I can't." I absentmindedly run my hand

over my bump. Pressing down in the usual spot, I'm rewarded with a small nudge from inside me. It makes me smile. "My shower is in a month and people need time to plan. Besides, we're five minutes away and Lauren has Heath's giant truck with her. We'll mow down anyone who gets in our way."

From the couch adjacent to me, Lauren giggles. She tried to get out of driving the truck she refers to as "the monster" so she could bring her roommate's car instead, but her boyfriend wouldn't hear of it. Something about safety being more important than style. I thought it was funny when she told me. Now, I should probably call and thank Heath. His giant truck will come in handy during this downpour.

Spence chuckles and I can't help but think about how lucky I am that he's so good to me. To us. Things could have turned out so much worse.

"Alright, alright. Just take it slow and I'll be there as soon as I can, okay?"

"We will. I promise. Text me when you get there and we'll meet you at the front so you can have your turn with the scanner gun."

"Will do. And take care of Baby Archie for me."

"We're not naming him after a prince," I argue. Again.

"He doesn't have a royal title so he's not a prince. Loveyoubye." Spence yells back and hangs up on me.

I stare at the phone, mouth agape.

"He got the last word in about the baby's name again, didn't he?" Lauren smiles as she lifts her travel cup of water to her lips.

"Every. Single. Time." I toss my phone on the couch and settle in. We still have some time before we have to leave for the appointment. "How's it feeling?" I gesture to Lauren's leg as she massages just above her knee. The tibia fracture that knocked her out of the entire gymnastics competition season last year is finally healed. But from the looks of it, it still bothers her. "Does it ache?"

"Mostly when it's going to rain."

"Or if you do too many tumbling passes?"

She crinkles her nose, knowing she's been caught. "Just don't tell my coach, okay?"

"You should be more worried about me telling Heath."

Lauren shrugs. "He's an athlete. What's he gonna say? 'Don't work out so hard'? He knows I'll throw that right back at him the next time he's bruised up from a game."

"This is why you two are perfect together. You understand each other."

"You have no idea," she murmurs and reaches over to the table, picking up a notebook.

I don't know that I'll ever understand how Heath and Lauren ended up together. Those two used to verbally spar with the best of them. But I suppose once your perception of someone changes, well, everything else changes too. Now they're what I like to refer to as a power couple—cheering each other on at every game or meet, pushing each other during workouts, making sure they're both stocked up in IcyHot and ibuprofen. It's fun to see Lauren happy and in love. She deserves it.

"I can't wait for you to see my new floor routine. *Christmas Eve Sarajevo* is amazing music for tumbling. And the turn sequence at the end makes me feel like I can do anything."

Thinking about the music, I can envision how Lauren turned such a powerful song into an equally powerful routine. For just a split second, it makes me yearn to dance again.

Then the moment is gone when Lauren flips open the cover of her notebook and poises her pen into the ready position. "Okay. Baby shower. I need a list of people to invite."

"Just do me one favor." She nods and gestures for me to continue. "My sister really wants to help. Or at least feel like she's helping. I know she's still in high school, but can you call her and ask her opinion on things? Just a couple of times."

Lauren doesn't skip a beat. "Of course. I'm glad Nicole is so excited. Is she going to be able to come?"

I shrug because I don't really know. "That's the million-dollar question. I'm almost positive my mom won't be there but I'm hoping she'll at least let Nicole come. Even if it's just to report back on how horribly bloated and exhausted I look and how much better off I would be if I'd just lived life their way in the first place."

Lauren laughs through her nose. "Sounds… stifling."

I shrug. "Their loss. Either they'll know their first grandchild or they won't. At this point, I don't really care."

I might eventually, but not today. Today is all about planning the celebration of my little boy's birth.

Lauren and I spend a good thirty minutes discussing baby shower guests and games. I try to veto the one where everyone has to cut off the same amount of ribbon as the circumference of my belly, but apparently, this isn't a democracy and she's going to do it anyway. As long as there's cake, I guess I'll survive.

"The only thing we need to really figure out is where to have this party," Lauren remarks as she continues jotting down ideas. "I don't know the area well enough so I might need to defer to you on this part."

"I bet the community group on social media would

know."

"You think?"

"Oh yeah. People are always asking for venues and specific businesses. Hang on."

I find the page I'm looking for and begin searching for a decent venue to hold a party. I know I've seen a whole thread about it before. But then one post in particular catches my eye.

CAUTION AVOID AVENUE R AT THE CORNER OF CINCINNATI. MAJOR ACCIDENT.

"Well shit," I grumble.

"What?"

"There's a car accident close to here. I think we have to go that way to get to the store. Let me see how long ago it was. Maybe it's cleared already. Otherwise, we need to go soon so we can find a way around it."

"Is it bad?"

"I can't tell yet. Just says its major."

I click on the post and my heart stops. A picture of the wreck has been posted in the comments and it looks like Spence's car. With a black sheet over it.

My breathing speeds up as I zoom in but can't see enough of the back window to tell if the spot in the bottom right corner is a promo sticker from his favorite radio station, or something else. Surely, it's something else. It's someone else's car. It can't be Spence's. I'm just overreacting. Mazda has lots of cars out there. Millions. It could be a million different people. Not my Spence.

The comments, though, do little to ease my mind.

It's going to be here a while, guys. An ambulance came out but they never took anyone away and they've stopped working. Pray for these people.

I'm here. Overheard an officer say they're waiting for the medical examiner.

Y'all pray for the families. That black sheet isn't a good sign. Usually that's only to cover the scene when someone has died.

"No, no, no, NO." My voice sounds shrill as I close the app and try to call Spence.

"Kiersten, what's wrong?"

I know Lauren is trying to talk to me, but I can barely hear her over the sounds of his phone ringing and my own heartbeat.

"Pick up, Spence. Come on, baby. Pick up."

Finally, someone answers. "Hey, this is Spence. You know what to do."

Dammit. I hang up, uninterested in leaving a voice message. I need to hear him, alive and breathing.

Dialing again, I continue my ministrations. "Come on, Spence. Answer the phone. Pull over if you have to. Please answer."

"Kiersten, what's wrong?"

I ignore her, waiting. Voicemail picks up again. I re-dial.

Small nudges begin pushing against my abdomen and I instinctually cradle my baby, our baby, as I try to reach his father. As I pray my life didn't just change forever because of a damn social media post.

"Come on, Spence," I say louder this time. "We need you, baby. Don't leave us. Answer the phone."

He never does.

TWO

Kiersten

Three years later

Our new place isn't huge, but it feels cramped with a toddler, three women, and two men—including a huge pro football player—standing in the living room. It doesn't help that we're surrounded by boxes.

I had to have all this help, though. It took all of us to move the never-ending piles of boxes without losing the toddler.

One exhausting day is nothing, though. I've lived through worse. Far worse. A cramped room and a long list of things to do is still a far cry from all the ugliness and despair I left behind. I'm choosing to focus on our new beginnings. I have a healthy son, a safe place to live, and good friends to help me move. Friends that have helped me get through the other crap I've been dealing with the last several years too.

Yeah. Life could be worse than being surrounded by people who love me.

"So, listen." Lauren plops down on the floor next to me and promptly yawns. We're exhausted from a full day of driving a moving truck and hauling furniture. If I never move again it'll be too soon.

"Heath and I were talking."

I look over at my best friend, a smirk on my face. Whenever she tells me they've been talking, that usually means they have an idea they want me to subscribe to.

Like the time they "talked about" me making a will and giving them custody of Carson if something were to happen to me.

Or the time they "talked about" paying the deposits and two month's rent on this apartment to make sure no one swooped in before I could get here.

Or the time they "talked about" co-signing on my car.

Admittedly, they were all really good ideas that I'm grateful for. "Leath," as I call them when they're not looking because they're basically a power couple, are just liars. They haven't been "talking about" anything. They've been "making decisions" on how to take care of me. No matter how much I protest, it won't do any good. Neither of them will back down. Lauren, because she loves me. Heath, because he loves my son. And I think he loves me, too. It took a while but we've found our footing as friends and pseudo-family.

"And what decision did you come to about my life this time?"

Lauren smiles sheepishly at me because she knows I'm right. She also knows I'm not angry about it. I never would have made it through the last three years without them. If anything, I'm embarrassed by how grateful I am.

"We want to help you pay for child care." I start to protest but she stops me quickly. "Not forever. Just until you get on your feet."

"Lauren, I appreciate it but I can afford it right now. I'm just doing drop-ins as needed."

"I know. But I also know your savings isn't going to last forever. You didn't get that much money from Spence's family." We both grimace at the thought of Wicked Witch Woodrow and her dancing monkey supporters who have made my life a living hell. "Heath and I would feel better if Carson could go to a good place at least part-time so he can make some friends and be social and stuff. He's going to need daycare when you work anyway. This just transitions him into it."

I sigh and drop my head back against the wall. "I really want to put my foot down, but I don't know how else to make it through all this right now. I know it'll get better when Carson is older and in school but—"

"But he's in diapers right now, Kiersten."

"Which I'm working on."

"Not the point right now. He'll get there," Lauren cuts in. "You're a single mom with zero support from your family. And Heath has a thirty-million-dollar contract with a twenty-mill signing bonus. It's not like we're stretching our budget to fit in daycare while you get settled."

"Remind me again why you work?"

Lauren raises her hand and I know she's about to tick off all the reasons on her fingers. "First of all…"

I snicker because I know her so well.

"… we're not married and I'll be damned if I'm going to shoot my future self in the foot by having a gap in my employment."

"Heath would never leave you."

"No, he wouldn't. But shit happens and I prefer to be prepared. Second," she continues, "I have way too much energy to stay home. I would die of boredom or Heath would kill me for following him around for some adult interaction. And last, one of the perks of being the office manager of a gymnastics training facility is getting to work out with the team a couple of nights a week."

"That's a definite bright spot."

"Beats the hell out of spending my evenings in step aerobics or on a treadmill."

The thought of her trying to keep herself entertained with your normal, average exercise classes amuses me. She'd rather pull her own toenails out with pliers and I know how much she wants to mess up her freshly pedi'd toes. Lauren needs hardcore exercise. Preferably the type that comes with bruises and battle scars. I understand completely. I'd rather take a dance class than weight training.

Sighing deeply, I let myself sink further into the floor as I observe the people who have become like family to me. Annika is unpacking the small kitchen, which isn't surprising. She's such a natural caretaker, I know it makes her feel like she's helping me by still going. And she's right.

Jaxon is resting on the couch after doing all the heavy lifting with Heath up a flight of stairs. I'm sure he's exhausted but I honestly think his laziness is more because he's being entertained by watching his best friend wrestle around with my son.

Carson's giggles fill the room as everyone relaxes and enjoys the show. His chubby little self keeps running at Heath who is laying on the floor on his back. Whenever he's close enough to grab, Heath tosses Carson in the air then puts him down and they start it all over again. My baby is going to sleep good tonight.

"Look at those two," Lauren says gently, just as entranced in the scene as I am. "That boy loves his Uncle

Heath, doesn't he?"

"So much," I agree quickly.

My son and her boyfriend have always been close. Maybe it's because Heath has several younger siblings, or maybe he's just a sucker for a cute baby, but from the second he held a three hours old Carson, they've had a really solid bond. It helps that Carson is a rough and tumble kind of kid. They can both get some energy out.

"I'm kind of glad we're living here now, just so Carson can get some more guy time." I stretch out my still cramped legs and cross them in front of me. "I feel like an ass for almost expecting it from Heath, but even just our regular hang out days is more male attention than he's ever gotten."

"You don't need to feel like as ass. Heath already went out and bought a toddler bed."

I turn my head to look at her, eyes wide in question. "Are you serious?"

Lauren giggles and pulls her knees to her chest, resituating herself. "He saw it at the store and had to get it. Said he just knows Carson will need to spend the night sometimes and wants him to have his own space."

"He said that?"

"That Carson needs his own space? He sure did. Even bought matching Paw Patrol sheets and a blanket, basically the whole set."

I press my lips together trying not to laugh. "Um, he knows Carson is a co-sleeper, right? That I've tried every which way to get him to sleep in his own bed but he refuses. It's best to just give up and tuck him in next to you until he falls asleep."

"Oh, he knows. Which is why I'm glad for our California king bed. I have a feeling he'll be bunking with us for a couple of years when he visits."

The thought of Carson in between Heath and Lauren in bed makes me laugh. They have no idea that this kid suctions to me like an amoeba and he's a kicker. I guarantee Lauren will be the one using that Paw Patrol bed after a couple of hours and a foot in the back.

Hopefully, all the wrestling happening now will knock Carson out enough that I can try putting him in his own bed. We set it up right next to mine. Maybe it'll work with me that close.

Wishful thinking, but these days, all I have are wishes and a few dreams.

"How come I'm the only one still unpacking?" Annika drops down on the other side of me.

"You're not. You're sitting like we are," Lauren smarts off.

"Now I am. I'm tired and I didn't even have to be up early this morning to drive a truck."

"Don't remind me." I roll my head trying to stretch out my shoulders and neck. "I didn't expect it to be that hard to drive a U-Haul."

"Or that long. It should never take more than two and a half hours to get from the western outskirts of Houston to the eastern outskirts of San Antonio," Lauren adds.

"How long did it take y'all?"

"Almost three and a half."

Lauren starts giggling next to me, which of course makes me laugh, too. "It would have been faster if you knew how to drive a stick."

That makes me laugh even harder. "They told me it would be a manual transmission."

"A stick *is* a manual transmission," Lauren half yells, unable to control her laughter.

"I didn't know," I protest. I thought they meant, like, I had to read the manual first or something."

Saying it out loud makes me realize exactly how stupid my mistake was. But if I've learned anything since Carson was born, you have to laugh at the little things, even major irritations, or else you'll spend your whole life crying.

The three of us crack up until tears roll down our faces and we can get our breathing back under control. I hope this is what it's like living here permanently now—all of us hanging out for barbecues and birthdays. All the events I should be spending with my family. Because that's what we are now. At least in my mind.

Don't get overzealous Kiersten. They have their own families, too. You're still in this alone.

The thought is sobering, but I can't fall into the trap of relying on anyone else. It's better to be surprised and relieved than disappointed and scrambling. Besides, Carson isn't their responsibility. He's mine. My biggest priority is making sure he grows up happy and healthy.

"Are you ready?" I ask Annika, smacking her lightly on the leg.

She smiles and bites her lip, an obvious sign of how happy she is. "I can't believe the wedding is finally almost here. It seems like I've been planning this thing for forever."

"It feels like it," Lauren agrees. "Figuring out bridesmaid dresses alone took weeks."

Annika shakes her head and blows out a breath. "I know a wedding is supposed to be a once-in-a-lifetime event and the end will be worth it, but I almost ditched the whole thing and went straight to the courthouse. I'm not girly enough for taffeta and lace."

"Thank goodness you've got a bestie over there who

knows how to do all those things." I gesture to Lauren who bats her eyelashes at us.

"No kidding. I love my dad but picking out a wedding dress with him was off the table before I even got engaged."

"Well thank goodness it's almost here. Just one week and you'll be Missus Jaxon Hart."

Annika looks at me like I've lost my mind. "Um, no. I'll be Ms. Annika Hart, thank you very much. I understand I'm marrying into a legacy but I refuse to ride on the coattails of my father-in-law or my husband. I've worked too damn hard to get where I'm at.

Just then, the groom-to-be pops up off the couch and walks by us, "You don't have to worry about that," he says and heads toward the front door. "No one will ever question your creditably as a trainer on that field, no matter what last name you have."

"Damn straight," Annika says strongly with a nod.

"Besides, if anyone gives you grief, I'll have my daddy fire them," Jaxon jokes making Lauren and I laugh.

Annika doesn't find it nearly as funny. She swipes at his leg while she bitches at him. "It's not too late to cancel your wedding, buddy."

"You would never! You love me too much." Jaxon grabs Annika's hands, pulling her to her feet for a quick kiss before smacking her on the ass. They're so damn cute together. It makes my heart squeeze with a mixture of happiness for them and a little bit of jealousy for me.

"Come on, y'all," Jaxon instructs. "Let's get the rest of this stuff unloaded. We need to get that U-Haul back and we all know it's going to take Kiersten an hour to drive it five miles to the drop-off site."

"Har, har," I laugh humorlessly and push up off the

floor. "I'm never living this down."

He's not wrong, though. We're running out of time. After a quick stretch and a little more bitching, we all get back to work.

THREE
Paul

Wiping down the bar, I glance around the room for the umpteenth time. Not that there's much more I can do. The wedding planner made sure all the decorations were put up this morning, the caterer is busy with last minute food preparations in the rarely used kitchen, and the wedding cake is being set up on the far side of the room. Even the DJ is almost completely set up. Everything is ready to go.

Still, it's the first big event I've hosted since purchasing this joint and I really want it to go well. Not just because my reputation is on the line, but because it's Jaxon and Annika's big day.

Jaxon didn't work for me too long, but we've kept in touch over the years. When he came to me and asked about renting out my place for his wedding reception, I immediately questioned his sanity. For all practical purposes, this place is still trying to figure out what it wants to be. Hell, I'm still trying to turn a profit. But Jax assured me the wedding planner would turn my small business into a reception worthy space. I finally said yes.

He was right. With a little TLC and fancy decorations, this place looks like a million bucks. It's a mixture of classy and country. Classy provided by the twinkle lights, cloth table coverings, and perfect centerpieces. Country provided by the general motif.

Our regulars wouldn't recognize the place if they walked in right now. Not that they'll ever see it. A private event will bring in a hell of a lot more money than the customers who call this place home and honestly, I can use the financial breathing room. Trying to turn a fledgling business into a success isn't as easy as it looks on television. I'm determined to succeed though. It's just a little rough around the edges and could use some improvements, but it's got good bones. And even more importantly, it's mine.

Two months later, and I still can't believe I bought a bar. It was never my dream growing up. For years I assumed I'd get a business degree and spend my adult years behind a desk of some corporate conglomerate wearing an ugly tie. In my mind, that was the definition of success. It wasn't until I got my first job as a bar back that my goals started to evolve.

During those years, I found that I enjoy working nights. My body likes sleeping during the day, so I always feel somewhat refreshed. As a man of few words, this environment seems to suit me. Turns out listening to people while behind a bar is my strong suit and comes easily. Conversations aren't ever long. Except for a few people, they also aren't in-depth. Even the ones who are using their bartender as a therapist aren't bad. If they get too intense or I don't care to hear any more, I can walk away during the conversation because I still have a job to do. Bar patrons seem to understand that better than say, retail customers.

Eventually, I realized my business instincts would carry me further than the few business classes I took, so I dropped out of college and spent my time learning the business from the ground up, working every position, and picking the brain of every general manager I worked under.

I purposefully worked my way up from the very bottom and I'm glad I did. Personally, I think it's part of what makes me good at my job. I understand the ins and outs. I know how difficult the various jobs can be and what can and can't be done in particular situations. I think it makes me able to assess my employees more objectively and keeps me from getting too heavy-handed.

Eventually, the opportunity to come here presented itself and I couldn't turn it down. I'm sure to others it seemed like a step backward but that's not how I saw it. This small non-descript hole in the wall business was my opportunity to take years of ideas, years of knowledge and use them to make what used to be called Sante a success. That's why Pat, the previous owner, hired me. He'd spent his life loving this place and wanted to make it profitable once again.

Unfortunately, he wasn't willing to let go of his old school ideas to let me get it there, nor would he invest any of the money necessary to bring the place into the current century. Or hell, even the last. Within six months he'd given up and decided he was ready for retirement. That's when he came to me with an offer I couldn't refuse.

Now I'm the proud owner of a bar-slash-dance hall.

The multiple personalities are part of what I'm working on fixing. The whole place is a little out there and doesn't seem to fit one particular demographic, which I suspect is part of why clientele is lacking. Is it a honky-tonk bar? Is it a dance club? Is it a concert venue? I suppose it depends on the night. But I need to streamline it a bit. Make it more marketable and classier, yet still have the down-to-earth feel. I have lots of ideas about the direction I could go, I just haven't found the one that "fits."

Yet another reason I'm glad to host this wedding reception. Not only am I helping a friend and buying myself a little time to make some decisions, I also want to see the reaction of people who've never been here before—what they like, what they turn their nose up at, what they complain about. I plan to do a little market research while they're here. Maybe it'll help me finally nail down a course of action. Failure is not an option when it comes to this business.

"Desiree," I call out to tonight's bartender and flip the towel into the bucket beneath the bar. "We stocked up on everything?"

She flashes me the same grin she uses with our customers. "We're good boss."

I haven't gotten to know Desiree well. Our shifts usually didn't overlap before. She's worked here for a while though and Pat never had any complaints about her work ethic, so that was good enough for me. I've been busy sorting through paperwork and doing behind the scenes things like inventory and cleaning out the apartment in the back so I could live on the property. I haven't made the effort with her I need to make.

For now, as long as she's running up the tabs with no complaints from the customers, she can keep doing whatever she's doing. The rest will come later.

"Good," I say with a nod and yet another glance around the room. "Please make sure to stay ahead of our stock and let me know if we're even getting remotely close to running out of anything. This isn't going to be like our regular nights. They'll be drinking faster and a lot more than normal. I don't want to leave anyone in waiting."

"Relax, boss. I got it." She flips her blonde hair over her shoulder (that she brags is in the realm of "the bigger the hair the closer to God"), as she heads to the other side of the bar, leaving me to blow out a breath.

She's right. I do need to relax. I've never been this nervous about an event before. I've also never been the one totally and completely accountable for its success before. Sure, the catering company and wedding planner will bear some of the responsibility should things go south, but realistically it's on me. It feels like my entire future as a business owner is on the line.

"Tammy!" I yell to the waitress who is doing one last quick wipe down of the tables. She's a couple of decades older than me and still loves working here. She's also quick on her feet so I love her being here. "We good?"

She flings her bright red hair over her shoulder and gives me a thumbs up. "Ready to go," she calls back and not a second too soon. The door swings open and people begin pouring in dressed in their wedding finest.

The wedding planner, whose name escapes me, hustles to the door and begins greeting people. I stand back, just watching and keeping a close eye for wedding crashers. I don't anticipate any, but Jaxon and Annika are no strangers to the press. They had quite the public love story and none of us would put it past some of the so-called "journalists" out there to sneak in for some exclusive pics. That's one of the reasons this place was a great option for them. Unless you know the address, you can't just search up *Frui Vita* and find it. I changed the name a few weeks ago and Google maps hasn't figured it out yet. That'll definitely be a problem later on, but today it works to our benefit.

Everyone must have caravanned from the wedding site because soon enough there's close to a hundred people hanging out. The drinks are flowing, the tables are being claimed, and everyone seems to be having a good time. So far, so good.

"Mr. Franklin." I turn at the sound of my name and come face to face with a mammoth of a man. His dark blond hair isn't spiky like all the pictures from back in the day. It's longer, despite a more receding hairline. Even with the crows' feet creasing his eyes, his size leaves no doubt he's still a force to be reckoned with.

"Mr. Hart," I say and put my hand out for him to shake. Jason takes it, his fingers literally engulfing mine. His grip is strong, probably from years of using the muscles in his fingers throwing a football. I'm not a small man. I cross the six-foot threshold and played ball back in my day as well. But standing next to the legend, Jason Hart, I look like a teenager. "Is everything to your liking so far? I made sure to stock up on the top-shelf liquor you requested and should have more than enough champagne for the toast with lots of extra for celebrating."

"First, please call me Jason. I realize I'm older than seventy-five percent of the people in this room, but I like to pretend I'm still young, and addressing me by my last name ruins the effect."

I chuckle in appreciation. I may only be thirty-five, but the years seem to be going faster these days. "Understood. Then please call me Paul. With as long as I've known Jaxon, I feel like we should all be on a first-name basis."

"Agreed." He reaches into the inner pocket of his suit and pulls out a couple of envelopes. "I know this party is only beginning but I wanted to make sure to take care of tipping everyone before the drinks really start flowing. I'd feel horrible if I forgot and being the father of the groom, well, no telling how many shots I'll have. Just don't tell the missus." He smiles conspiratorially at me and I have a feeling this has been a topic of conversation in their household leading up to the wedding. "How many of the employees here are yours?"

"The catering company brought all their people. I'm just responsible for the other bartender Desiree and Tammy over there." I point to the redhead as she places some specialty drinks down on the table in front of her. The guests look pleased as they take their first sips which is exactly what I was hoping to see. "She'll be mostly bussing tonight and some waitressing. Whatever you guys need just let one of the three of us know. We've got it covered."

"Will do. And do you mind giving these to your employees before they leave tonight?"

He hands me the envelopes and I take a quick peek inside so I know what to prepare for. There are several hundred-dollar bills is each of them. Stunned, I quickly close them not wanting to accidentally flash this amount of cash around. "I don't understand. They have the tip jars already set up."

"This is my son's wedding and you guys are going to be busting your tails when this group gets going. You'll just have to take my word for that." He smiles again and I have no doubt tonight is going to end with a lot of fun stories and at least one puker. I should probably get the mop ready just in case. "I want to make sure the effort is worth it for the people working."

"That's really nice of you." I think about Tammy who I know lives paycheck-to-paycheck and how much this will mean to her. This, on top of the tip jar people will be sure to fill up tonight, is going to make a big difference. "I'll make sure they get it after everyone heads out for the night. But I only have two employees, so I don't need this one."

I try to hand back the extra envelope, but Jason holds up his hand. "You're working just as hard as they are. If you don't want to keep it for yourself, just consider it payment for the extra booze you had to order. I know you're just starting out and I know how important you are to my kids. Man," he wipes his hand down his face. "I have another kid. I have a daughter-in-law now. How weird is that?"

Even with as long as he's had to prepare, he looks shellshocked by his own news. "She's a really nice woman. I'm glad they found each other."

"Me, too." He knocks on the bar twice and nods. "Thanks again, Paul."

Turning to walk back to his guests, Jason throws his massive arms out wide as he makes a joke about his own wedding day. I don't stick around to hear the punchline. Instead, I head for the back to put this cash in the safe. By the end of the night, there will be more in the register, but I still don't want Desiree and Tammy to see yet.

Quickly and mostly out of curiosity, I count out each envelope.

A thousand dollars apiece. That's easily a couple of weeks' worth of tips in one night. If I only had a pro athlete or two pop in a couple of nights a week, this place would be profiting in no time.

The thought makes me stumble as my ideas begin taking over. What if… what if I catered to the sports teams in the area. We have football, basketball, baseball, and a hockey team all within twenty-five miles of each other. All have athletes that make a shit ton of money. And I'm willing to bet they could use an out of the way place that is hard to find where they can hide out to decompress without fear of their faces being splashed all over social media. I have no idea how I'd get the word out to them, but it's something to think on.

The idea continues to percolate as I lock the safe and head back to the front, getting back to work. As I scan the crowd, I notice at least two San Antonio Steer players, not to mention a number of retired athletes milling about.

The whole reason Jaxon asked if his reception could be held here is because of the privacy. Could this be the answer? Could the off the beaten path location and lack of marketing work to my advantage? Could I cater to professional athletes and give them a place to just relax?

I tuck the thought into the far corners of my brain when the crowd erupts into cheers as the happy newlyweds walk through the front door. I join the celebration when Jaxon and Annika raise their clasped hands in a victorious gesture.

I'm happy for them. They deserve all the happiness in the world and the excitement on their faces makes me believe they've found it. But how could they not? Jaxon's a good guy, comes from money, is working hard through medical school. He's got so much to offer an amazing woman like Annika. He's the kind of guy who deserves to get the girl in the end so they can have their happily ever after.

Me? I'm the kind of guy who works too hard, has almost nothing to his name, and refuses to give up on a dingy bar. The idea of a relationship, someone to partner with me in life is a deep longing. Deep enough I don't consciously remember it's there most days. But it's not in the cards for me. My life was never set up for me to be a good partner in return. Maybe it's best that I keep my focus solidly on my new business.

Decision made to enjoy Jaxon's happiness instead of focusing on me, I join Desiree behind the bar to help get this party started.

FOUR

Kiersten

Dropping down on the barstool, I peel my heels off my poor, aching feet. This reception has turned into the party of the year, and it just confirms to me that I made the right choice uprooting myself and moving here. It's further away from my sister, who I miss terribly, but there were too many reasons to leave.

Not that I need to think about those right now. I'd rather concentrate on the little stinker across the room being tossed into the air by his Uncle Heath. My boy's giggles are permeating the room and I'm not the only one watching.

Smiling at their interaction, I think about how it sucks that Carson doesn't have a father. I never wanted that for him. But Heath has been the best stand-in we could ask for. I have no doubt Lauren's beau will show up with her for every t-ball and flag football game Carson ever plays. To be honest, I won't be surprised if he coaches some of those teams as well.

He's not the only one. Over the last few years, Jaxon

and Annika have been like family too. More like an extended family type role due to our mutual friendship with my childhood bestie, but we've fallen into our own solid relationships as well.

"All the single ladies out there," the DJ calls through the microphone and I immediately begin plotting my escape because I know what's coming. "I need y'all to gather up here for the bride to toss her bouquet."

I groan and quickly look around, wondering if I have time to hide out in the restroom. It's my only chance. Popping off the stool I try to make a break for it, but I'm too late.

"Oh no you don't." Lauren threads her arm through mine and tugs. "I know we hate these things because they're misogynistic, outdated, and feel like way too much pressure on a topic we both despise, but Annika absolutely loathes them. The least we can do is make it quick and painless for her."

I huff, but allow myself to be guided away, leaving my heels behind for now. "There is no such thing as painless when it comes to this antiquated tradition."

"True." Lauren weaves us through the small crowd trying to get to the front. "But there is safety in numbers so don't leave my side."

We finally push through the people to get into position and I almost laugh at the look on Annika's face. It's painfully obvious she's trying to be a good sport but this clearly wasn't her idea. My money is on the wedding planner forcing the issue. She put together a damn good wedding, but Lauren has complained about her pushy nature from day one. I thought Lauren was just trying to force her own ideas into the planning mix since Annika has almost no opinions about things like decorations and centerpieces, but judging by Annika's expression, I may have misjudged.

At least she looks beautiful. Her dress is gorgeous but not overstated. The corseted tulle A-line gown with a cascading skirt is more of a silver color than white. Her dark hair looks delicately pinned in the back, even though I'm sure it's secured in a hundred different places, allowing her long curled locks to tumble down her shoulders and back. The whole look is stunning but doesn't take away from who she is—the newest intern in the training department for the San Antonio Steer and tomboy at heart. Hence why there are so many football players crowding the floor as they wait for their turn.

I sigh as we wait for the last of the single women to reach the small dance floor. There are quite a few of us, most of them the "plus one" of one of the guys. And of course, Jaxon's twelve-year-old sister, Lucy. I'm more than happy to jump out of the way if the bouquet comes in her direction. I'm positive at her young, unjaded age she has more romantic bones than I do.

Finally, we're ready and the DJ quickly does his spiel.

"If the new Mrs. Jaxon Hart would do us the honor of turning around."

I bark out a laugh at him calling her that. If she wasn't in her wedding dress, I'd bet money Annika would throw the bouquet in his face for using Jaxon's name instead of hers. But being the blushing bride she is, she follows his instructions and on the count of three, the flowers go sailing over her shoulder.

I wish I could say it went in slow motion until some smiling, excited woman caught it, delight written all over her face. That's not how it happens at all.

Annika throws it hard with no arch whatsoever, more

like a missile shooting straight into Lauren's arms.

She looks down at the petals in disbelief. When reality finally hits, she immediately follows up with a "son of a bitch."

The DJ continues with whatever he does during this game, but I'm not listening. I'm too busy laughing at Lauren. Annika seems just as thrilled by this turn of events as I am.

I pat Lauren on the forearm and give her a "good luck" before heading back to my post at the bar.

"Sorry about your defeat," the beautiful bartender says wistfully, as if catching a bouquet is really an indicator of your own pending marriage. "What can I get ya?"

"Can I get a dirty martini? Extra dirty, please."

"You got it."

I make a quick glance around to find my son who has apparently been passed off by Heath to the father of the groom while all the single men get ready for the garter toss. I'm not surprised Carson looks perfectly content. Pushing three years old, he's never met a stranger. It's a great quality for him to have, and yet it terrifies me on a regular basis. If I didn't know Heath would step in front of a moving bus for my kiddo, I'd be more concerned by a man I've only met a handful of times taking over baby duty.

Letting my body sink onto the stool, I take advantage of just being able to sit. Carson runs me ragged every day but pounding the pavement for the last week or so has added an extra element of exercise I haven't had in a long time.

Unfortunately, the health benefits are the only thing I got out of it. No one was hiring. I hit as many dance studios as I could find in a ten-mile radius and they all said the same thing—they're fully staffed now but they'll be hiring for summer. I appreciate that more than one of them said they would call if they have an opening, but that doesn't help me now.

"Hey, Desiree." The red-headed waitress comes flying up to the bar. "I need a strawberry margarita, an Old Fashioned, and a Bloody Mary, stat." Her hands fly as quickly as her words as she unloads some dirty glasses from her tray onto the rubber mat on the bar.

Desiree just nods and places my dirty martini in front of me before heading straight back to mixing.

It's odd that the waitress just blurted out an order. As I look around more, I realize the only register they have is behind the bar. There's no computer system. It's straight up old school here. That's kind of cool, actually. Gives the place an interesting feel.

As I watch them continue with their respective job duties, another thought occurs to me.

"Are there only two of you working tonight?" I ask, not because I'm making conversation but because I have an idea and I'm kind of an opportunist at this point.

The waitress looks up, almost surprised to notice me sitting here. "Us? Oh yes. The caterer brought everyone else. Only three people work here full time, including the owner. It's all hands on deck tonight."

I sip my cocktail with appreciation. It's the right amount of dirty for me. "Only three *total*? For a place this size?"

"Well, we normally don't have this many customers. And not a lot of people come in looking for work at an out-of-the-way place like this that doesn't line their pockets with Jacksons." She wipes down her tray and places it on the counter, ready to be filled with fresh drinks. "Why? Looking for a job?"

Swallowing another sip, I carefully place the glass

down and grab the cocktail pick holding two olives. "Actually, I am."

Her eyebrows raise slightly with interest. "Really. You ever worked at a bar before?"

I shake my head and snag an olive with my teeth. "Nope."

"Got any waitressing experience?"

Another shake. "Nope. But I spent several years as a dance instructor. I also have solid references, three years of college under my belt, and a working car. Does any of that help?"

She smiles at me and ducks under the counter to the other side of the bar. Riffling around on the shelves for a second, she finally pulls out what she's looking for and places it in front of me.

"This has been back here for a while and we're under new management so the application is kind of old, but it should do the trick. We could use some fresh blood around here."

Now it's my turn to raise my eyebrows.

"Don't ask." She shoots a glance over at the bartender. Clearly, there is no love lost there. She ducks back under the bar and makes her way to my side. "The boss is great, the pay is fair, and it's not terribly stressful. Just give that to me when you're done. Need a pen?" Before I can respond she grabs one out of her hair and hands it to me. Just as I go to take it, a thirty-pound tornado runs right into my legs.

"Mama!" he squeals and hugs me so tightly, I can't even pick him up. All I can do is rub his little back and tell him I love him before he's off like a shot, chasing after Lucy, who seems to be just as enamored with him as he is with her.

The waitress nods toward Carson. "Working in a bar means being here for weird shifts. You sure you wanna do this?"

"Under the circumstances, yes. And rest assured, I have a remarkably strong support system."

And that system started putting things in place for us before the first whine of the U-Haul's gears. The daycare Lauren and Health found is really nice. Clean and bright, and the teachers were all lovely when we toured the place. I verified that they have a low-income program which will help me out when the time comes. If it comes. Assuming Uncle Heath hasn't already told them to bill him for everything. Wouldn't surprise me if years down the road I find out Carson has a college fund, too.

I know him being so actively involved with caring for my son would seem weird to some people, but I'm just grateful. Heath is a natural protector and provider. I can't begrudge my son being the recipient of it, even if it seems a bit unconventional. Besides, kids are a long way down the road for them. If this is how Heath gets his baby fever out of his system, so be it.

"You'll need all the help you can get with these hours. Names Tammy, by the way." She sticks her hand out and I shake it quickly. It's boney, matching her equally thin frame, but she's got a solid grip. If I had to guess it's from years of manual labor. She may be significantly older than the beautiful young bartender, but I'm willing to bet Tammy will last a lot longer on the job.

Desiree takes that moment to deliver Tammy's drink order, without so much as glancing her way. The vibe confirms my initial impression that these two don't get along. At all.

Tammy hikes up the tray in front of her and pats me on

my shoulder. "Just get that to me when you're done and I'll make sure the boss man sees it."

I smile with gratitude at her kindness. This kind of work wasn't my goal, but my savings account won't last forever. A job is a job at this point.

Despite the line of a dozen or so customers waiting for service, Desiree comes over and begins wiping down the counter. It's already clean so I suspect she's got something to say.

"You know he's not hiring, right?" Her tone is haughty and teeters on combative.

I shrug, hoping to de-escalate the aggression she's clearly trying to throw my way. "Neither is anyone else. I'm filling out as many applications as I can. You never know when someone is going to quit, right?"

She narrows her eyes at me but doesn't say anything else, instead being called over to the other end by the man I assume is the big boss. If I'm not mistaken, he looks a bit irritated she was "cleaning" instead of paying attention to the customers. Interesting. Maybe this application won't be a waste of time after all.

FIVE
Paul

When Pat hired me, this place was named Sante. No one seemed to know where the name came from, not even Pat.

I thought it was supposed to mean "cheers" in Spanish, but without an accent mark over the e, it was spelled wrong anyway. It drove me crazy and felt like a bad omen to have a typo in the original name, so I changed it before the ink was dry on the business papers.

We now work at Frui Vita, which means "enjoy life" in Latin. That's what I want people to do here—enjoy themselves. I want every customer to walk out with a smile on their face and a good memory to take with them. And I don't want any more typos on the sign outdoors.

I also don't want to keep trying to figure out why these books don't balance.

"Fuck." I toss the papers on my desk and dig the heels of my hands into my eye sockets until I see stars.

Math shouldn't be this hard. This isn't calculus. Still, I can't figure out why we're spending this much money on liquor. I know we don't have enough customers to be drinking this much. Either someone is stealing bottles behind my back, or the bartenders are making extra strong drinks.

I suspect it's the latter since I'm the only one with a key to the liquor closet. That means I'm going to have to retrain my employees and I don't have the time or desire to do that. Tammy and Desiree have been working here for years. Hell, I worked alongside them. They should know better.

"Knock, knock." Speaking of Tammy.

"Hey, yeah," I wave her over. "Come on in. You getting ready to open up shop?"

"Already did." She drops down into the chair in front of my desk. "No one's here yet. I thought I'd check on you and see how it's goin' on with the back end of things."

Tammy's Texas accent is strong. I don't know if it's because she was born and raised in the Lone Star State or if she plays it up for show, but it works for her. In her mid-50s, Tammy's curly red hair is piled on top of her head, the lines on her face an indicator of a life hard lived. And probably hard loved. Married for at least two dozen years, she's as committed to her man now as she was the day she got hitched—or so she says.

"It's…" I start, trying to come up with some sort of answer that isn't negative. There's no point in lying to Tammy though. She has a knack for seeing right through me. Instead, my shoulders slump and I tell her the truth. "…rough. We need some regulars."

"We've needed new regulars for years. Those bastards stopped tipping when they decided I was their friend more than their waitress."

I sigh deeply. I knew taking over the bar would be

rough, but I didn't realize it had gotten worse for them as well. I was hoping the Hart reception would be a tipping point in the right direction, but it didn't stretch us as far as I'd hoped.

All my life it's been drilled into me that success is the only right answer. The idea of potential failure causes my teeth to clench and blood to run cold through my veins. I'll do anything necessary to keep this bar up and running, even taking suggestions from my employees.

"Got any ideas?"

"Sure. Fire Desiree."

I choke back a laugh at her unexpected outburst. "Excuse me? I thought you liked working with her."

Tammy purses her lips. "I don't know where you got that idea. I like working nights, not working with her. First time in my life the husband and I are working the same hours. It's amazing what some regular hanky-panky can do for your mood."

"Okay," I interrupt loudly, not at all interested in hearing more about Tammy's sex life. "Enough of that. Why do you think she should be fired?"

"Easy," she says with a shrug. "That girl is unreliable and probably a functional alcoholic."

I hold my hands up to stop her. "Whoa, whoa, whoa. I might give you unreliable since she's late for her shifts fairly regularly, and yes, she's called in a time or two. But functional alcoholic? Are you sure? I've never seen her take so much as a sip of the booze here."

"That's 'cause you're a hot piece of man candy, so she doesn't do it in front of you. Wants to keep up appearances so she pretends to be a hard worker and all that. But she probably goes through half a bottle of Jack every night just taking shots with the customers *in solidarity*," she says with air quotes, "for whatever problem they have going on that night."

I sit back in my squeaky chair, stunned by this revelation. I always assumed Desiree was a little scatterbrained but ignored it because the customers seem to like her well enough. Now I'm wondering if we've got an even bigger problem with her working here. First and foremost, not smart for someone with a potential drinking problem to be responsible for mixing and serving drinks. Not to mention the liability I'd have if she were to drive home and hurt someone.

At least one mystery is solved though.

"This is probably why we're spending more on liquor than we should be. If she's tipsy she is probably overpouring."

"That's my guess," Tammy says without the slightest hint of guilt for ratting out her co-worker. "Pat kept saying he was going to put a stop to it, but then Desiree would flash her big smile and shimmy her big boobs and he'd melt into a perverted little puddle."

"Pat knew?" I ignore the comment about his perversion. That's the least shocking part of her revelations tonight.

Tammy shrugs again. It's amazing how sometimes she truly does not give a shit what anyone thinks of her. Probably why she's such a good employee. "Call him and ask him."

I pinch between my eyes. "No. I believe you. Everything you're saying makes sense. It just sucks that I have to get rid of someone who's already trained and find someone new."

"Oh. Well, that's easy," Tammy says excitedly. The about-face is so sudden, I actually startle. "A girl was at that wedding reception looking for work. Real cute. Seems reliable. Not a hint of booze on her. Well, except for the dirty martini she was drinking, but she was a guest."

I snort a laugh. "Not drunk at noon. Always good in a prospective employee."

"It was evening. Plus, beggars can't be choosers, boss. I left her application on your desk." Tammy reaches over and sorts through my scattered pile. It's a wonder she can find it in this mess. "Here it is. Kiersten Willoughby. Oooh." She waggles her eyebrows. "She has a fancy name."

"I don't care what her name is as long as she can do the job. Hand it over."

I snatch the resume from Tammy's hands and glance over it. It looks like most of her employment history is being a dance teacher. No bar experience whatsoever, but she had a fast food stint in high school for a while. It's something anyway.

"At least she has a steady employment history. That's a plus, I suppose," I say under my breath, more to myself than my waitress.

"Wait 'til you meet her. She's sharp. Don't know why she wants to work in a bar—"

"Hey!" I protest, which Tammy ignores.

"—But you don't want to miss this one. My gut says what she doesn't know she'll pick up quickly. I'm surprised you didn't notice her. Real pretty girl."

I take a second to think through the guests that night. There were a lot people and I was so focused on making a good impression, I didn't really pay much attention to anything beyond serving up drinks.

Looking at the application again, I realize Tammy is right. I don't know why she wants to work here with all this dance experience but I'm not here to judge. As long as she can do the job and not steal my booze, it'll still be a better situation than I'm in now.

A loud cheer from the other room reminds Tammy and me of exactly why we're here.

"Sounds like our resident bartender has just had her first camaraderie shot of the night." Tammy pushes out of her seat and makes her way to the door. She points at me. "Call that girl. I'm not sure how much longer Desiree can pretend she's sober while she works."

With those parting words, Tammy exits the room and leaves me to my thoughts.

I glance down at my watch, noting it's only seven-thirty. Well past business hours if I worked in an office, but I don't. This is an after-hours establishment. If this Kristen, or however you say her name, is going to work here, she better get used to phone calls at weird times.

Grabbing my office phone receiver, I dial the number from the top of the paper.

It only takes a couple of rings before a gentle voice answers. My first thought is she's going to have to get a little more gruff if she's going to be effective behind a bar.

"Yeah, I'm looking for a, uh, Kristen Willoughby."

There's a pause on the other end of the line before she responds.

"This is Kiersten."

"Sorry. Anyway, *Kiersten*, this is Paul Franklin. I'm the owner of Frui Vita. It seems you dropped off an application with one of my employees during the wedding reception last week and she was really impressed with you."

"Oh, yes." Kiersten's voice immediately perks up. Maybe she doesn't need to get more gruff after all. "It looks like a neat place to work."

"Why?" I'm truly curious. It's just a bar. I'm working

on making it something better, but right now there's not really anything different about it than any other run-of-the-mill place.

"I guess I've always thought working at a bar looks interesting. Talking to the people. Learning how to make mixed drinks. Live music. It seems like every night would be different. I like that. I don't like it when things get boring."

I feel like there's a bit of desperation in her answer. Like she needs this job badly and is willing to kiss a little ass to get it. I'm oddly okay with that. I appreciate her trying to put her best foot forward. Combined with Tammy's initial impression, I think we may have found my newest employee. But I still need to ask a few important questions.

"Look Kiersten, I'm gonna cut to the chase. I need someone who will be here on time and work hard. I don't need a slacker or someone who is going to drink on the job."

"Understood."

"Do you have reliable transportation?"

"Yes, sir. I have a car. It's got some miles on it but I keep up with all the regular maintenance so it should last me a while."

"Perfect. We mostly serve beer on tap, but we also serve liquor. Can you make a mixed drink?"

"Just the basics. My friends say I make a mean margarita and I know how to make regular martinis. But I'm a fast learner," she adds in quickly.

"Last question. Are you a thief?"

"Uh… What?"

"Sorry, that came out wrong. Do you have a record for any kind of theft?"

"No. I don't have any kind of record at all. But since

you're leveling with me, I'll extend the same courtesy. I need this job too much to risk it by being a douchebag. If you hire me, I'll train hard and work even harder. As long as you're a good employer, I'm happy to be a good employee."

I find myself smirking at her candor. Tammy was right—she is impressive. Even over the phone.

"I like your style. And you're friendly enough. When can you start?

"Wait. You don't want to see me first?"

"I trust Tammy's recommendation. And I don't need to see you to know you're better than what I've got."

"Oh. That's kind of sad. But in that case, I'll start tomorrow."

We work out a few more details, including pay scale and the hours she'll work. By the time we hang up, I feel even more confident that Tammy was right on. I'll have to thank her later. Maybe someday I can even thank her with a raise.

Another cheer comes from the front and I have a bad feeling that was camaraderie shot number two. I can't afford any more of those tonight. It's time to put on my boss hat and fire my first employee.

This is going to suck.

SIX

Kiersten

In hindsight, I probably should have asked Lauren if she could babysit before agreeing to start a new job, but I was afraid the opportunity was going to slip through my fingers if I didn't take it right then.

It wasn't until I hung up that I thought about the fancy new daycare we'd already toured and that they close at six and aren't open on weekends. I looked into some other options, but I don't feel right about leaving Carson in a twenty-four-hour facility. Besides, the closest one is by the San Antonio airport and I'm nowhere near there. The only other option, at least until I come up with some other ideas, is letting Carson go to daycare in the afternoon with Lauren picking him up after work and keeping him until I'm home. I hate feeling like an imposition.

"Are you sure this is okay?" I hand Carson to my best friend, who begins peppering him with kisses making him giggle and squirm until she puts him down. He immediately takes off running to the toy box Lauren has hiding behind an oversized chair. "My new boss is training me to close. I won't be off until at least two. I might be as late as four. That's really early to wake you up."

That gets me an annoyed look. "Which is why you're going to go home and grab a few hours of sleep before I drop Carson off at your place on my way to work."

"What? You can't do that."

"Why not?"

"It's above and beyond." I cry indignantly, growing more and more uncomfortable with how much I'm coming to rely on her. This is why I refused to move in with them despite how much room they have. I didn't want them to become more responsible than they should be for me and my son. And yet, here I am.

"No, dragging my ass up at four a.m. only to try and fall back asleep for a few hours is going above and beyond, which is why it's not gonna happen. I'd rather not interrupt my REM cycle and as a bonus because of the great friend I am, you'll get one, too. It's not a big deal," she reiterates. "I'll leave for work at nine and with rush hour, it'll take me half an hour max to get to your place. That gives you a solid five hours of sleep before you have to wake up. And he still takes naps so as of today, you do too. And that's on the days Heath doesn't beg me to leave him here for a while. You can sleep as much as you want then."

I rub my forehead, willing my brain to come up with a solution that doesn't require my friends to become like my son's second parents.

"Listen, Kiersten, I know it's not ideal, but it's way better than never getting any rest at all."

I bite my lip, still hesitating, but she's right. This is better than any alternative, no matter how much I feel like I'm intruding on her life. "Are you sure? Like *really* sure."

"What's to be sure about? Heath isn't even here tonight. He's on a road trip with his dad and I'm already bored. Carson and I will eat some boxed mac and cheese, watch some cartoons and take a bath. Sounds like a perfect night."

It does sound pretty amazing. Now I wish I was the one staying home while she went to work. But I don't have time to dwell on what-ifs. It's depressing and there's no point in wishing for things that won't happen.

"Thank you." I lean in to give her a hug. Lauren has been my best friend since high school and I'm lucky to have her. Most friendships that start during the teen years dissolve when everyone leaves for college, but ours never did. Even with all the shit the teenage years and beyond has brought, we've always been this close. I'm excited to live in the same town as her again, not just because of the help she's offering, but because I get to see her on a regular basis.

Pulling back, she smooths down my hair. "No need to thank me. We're family. It's what we do. Now, where is my date for the night? Carson!"

"Lolo!" He yells back from behind the chair.

I laugh at his nickname for her. "Baby boy, Mommy has to leave."

We listen quietly, curious to hear what kind of response he's going to give. It takes a minute for him to decide.

"Okay bye!" he finally yells.

"Little twerp." I shake my head and go track him down so I can get at least one hug before I go. He's still behind the chair, but now he's inside the toybox. "What are you doing in there?"

Carson looks up at me with his wide eyes and shows me the cars he's holding in his hands. "Car, Mama. Pay car wif Unca Heat."

I snatch him out of the container and blow a raspberry on his neck. "I see you have cars. But Uncle Heath isn't here. You're going to have to play with Lolo while Mommy goes to work, okay?"

"Otay."

I could be sad that my baby doesn't seem concerned by me leaving, but more than that, I'm glad he feels comfortable here. It'll be much easier to calm myself down in the car than to calm us both in the doorway.

Setting him back on the floor next to the plethora of toys, way more than he needs if you ask me, I ruffle his dark hair.

"Welp, I guess I'm on my way."

Lauren grins at me and shakes her head. "He'll be fine. I'll make sure to text you four million times with updates so you feel better."

"I'd appreciate it."

She rolls her eyes and follows me to the door, making sure to lock it behind me as I leave.

This isn't a new thing. I've left Carson so I can work before. My sister, Nicole used to babysit him all the time. Somehow this feels different. This isn't just picking up shifts here and there as needed. This is a full-time position. I'll be missing his bath and bedtime five nights a week.

Settling into my five-year-old Honda Civic, I find myself wishing I could call my mother for advice or encouragement but there's no point. She'll just remind me again how this is the consequence of my own actions. I've heard it all from her before.

When Carson was first born, I expected it. I got pregnant in college by a guy I barely knew. Of course, she was going to have some judgmental things to say. I assumed at some point she'd let it go. Almost three years later it still hasn't happened. Except for a weekly phone call to make sure she's still in good health, we don't talk much at all.

The sad thing is, she doesn't need to remind me of my own choices because I live them every day. Hearing it over and over and *over* isn't doing anything except wasting her breath and all of our time. Plus, it takes away from Carson. If anyone is innocent in this difficult situation, it's him.

If only my mother could put down her pride long enough to see that she's missing out on the most wonderful grandson just to keep reminding me that she's "right."

Ironic since she's wrong.

Yes, being a poor single mom is my own damn fault. But I'd stay this way for the rest of my life to have my baby boy. He is the reason I get up in the morning and the reason I sleep well at night. I love my son more than I hate being poor. Too bad she can't see that through her lens of conservative consequences.

My phone rings on cue, as if my sister can hear me struggling with thoughts of my family. I know it is her without even looking. She always seems to know when I'm having a moment and wants to make me smile. Maybe she'll tell me something to brighten my day.

I quickly connect the Bluetooth. "Hey, stranger," I answer brightly as I drive through the residential neighborhood. I've got one pit stop to make before heading to work. "Are you almost ready for the college experience?"

At six years my junior, Nicole is just a couple weeks away from high school graduation. She toyed with spending the summer relaxing at home but is anxious to get out into the world by herself for the first time, so she opted to enroll in a summer program. It makes me nervous, not because she's young but because she's so damn sweet. She's the kind of girl who's never met a stranger and has a kind word and a smile for everyone. I'm pretty sure she's where Carson inherited his disposition from. I'm hoping she learned from watching my mistakes and knows how to stay out of some bad situations. Lord knows I've lectured her enough times it should all be engrained in her brain by now. Just in time for her to set out on her own.

"I've already started packing. I can't wait to get out of here. I love mom, but she is stifling sometimes."

That she is.

"She just wants to keep you from making the mistakes I did."

Nicole huffs. "I will never call my nephew a mistake. He's too stinkin' cute. How is he anyway? Tell me what I missed."

"That kid," I say with a chuckle as I pull into the drive-through of the post office. "He fell asleep on the couch last night so I put him in his new bed. In the middle of the night, I woke up and happened to look over. He was sitting straight up, glanced around for a second like he was in a daze and when he found me said, 'No mama. *My* bed!' Then he climbed into *my* bed and attached himself to me. I swear he has eight legs with suction cups sometimes."

Nicole laughs. "That sounds like him alright. Poor kid is going to be sleeping with you well into his teenage years."

"Poor kid? Poor me. If he gets any bigger, I'll fall off the bed for sure. As it is, I wake up hanging off the side."

She sighs deeply. "I miss him so much."

"I know. He misses his Nic-Nic, too. Hold on just a second. I need to drop these bills in the mailbox."

"Okay."

I count the envelopes quickly to make sure I haven't forgotten any. Yep, I've got all four. I sigh as I shove them in the slot and roll my window back up.

Time to hit the highway.

"Sorry. I'm back," I say to my sister as I look over my shoulder to get in the correct lane.

"It's no problem. But why are you mailing in your bills instead of doing it online?"

I run my hands through my hair before gripping the steering wheel a little harder than necessary. "This way buys me a few more days to get some more cash into the account to make sure it doesn't overdraft."

"Don't you have overdraft protection?"

"Yeah, but I need to keep that small nest egg in my savings. Tires for my car aren't cheap and I'll need them soon."

I can envision the frown she's wearing now. She worries about her big sister too much. "I get why you had to move away. It just sucks that you guys aren't here anymore."

"Not like you'll be there much longer. Just a couple more weeks and you'll be spreading your own wings. Besides, you'll come to visit right? Once we get a little more settled?"

"Of course, I will. He's got a birthday coming up in a couple of months. I wouldn't miss that for the world. Just make sure it's on a weekend."

"I will do my best," I say with a wide grin at the thought of her visiting my new home. "Hopefully we'll see you before then. If nothing else, we'll Skype in the next couple of days. You know how he loves that."

Exiting the highway, I pay close attention to the street names, looking for my turn.

"And I love seeing straight up his nose every time you walk away from the iPad. By the way, you need to clean your ceiling fans. I forgot to tell you that last time we talked."

"I do not," I say with a giggle. "I just moved in. They're fine."

"I don't know. I got a very long and close up view of them. It was a lot of fun to watch them spin while listening to Paw Patrol in the background."

"Okay, okay, I get it. I'll pay closer attention next time."

Finding the parking lot to Frui Vita, I pull in and take a space under a light in the middle.

"I don't mind just sitting there with him," she adds. "I just prefer to watch him, not your ceiling."

"You're a good auntie, Nic-Nic."

"And you're a good mom, KK."

Turning off my car, I grab my purse and toss my keys inside. "As much as I want to talk to you more, I just got to my new job so I need to go."

Nicole gasps. "You got a job? Why didn't you tell me?"

"Because it happened yesterday. Don't get all excited. I'm working at a bar. But I like the owner and the waitress seems really nice so I don't want to be late on my first day."

"I'm so happy for you. Call me when you can so you can tell me all about it. Maybe you'll meet a hunky customer and fall in love."

I snort a laugh. "In my experience, a bar is the last place I want to meet someone. But thanks for the good vibes. Go finish packing, baby sister. You have a dorm to move into."

"Will do. Love you."

"I love you, too."

We disconnect and I take a deep breath.

It's not my dream job, but it's gainful employment. Time to make a good impression.

SEVEN
Paul

iring Desiree wasn't as dramatic as I thought it would be. At first, she denied my claims of her drinking copious amounts on the job but the more I insisted I knew the truth, the less weight her rebuttals held. Finally, she admitted she'd done a couple of stints in rehab and apologized for her behavior.

It made me kind of sad to find out she has a serious problem with alcohol. It also made me question how deeply rooted the addiction is if she decided to work here. Did she think she could handle it or was it just a great way to have access to all the free booze she wanted?

I'm not sure, but it's also not something I can dwell on. I offered to help her find another rehab, but she didn't take me up on it. One thing I've learned from working in this industry as long as I have, you can't help an alcoholic. You can support one in their journey to health, but they have to do the work. The best way I could assist her in getting better is by taking her job away.

Of course, that means I have to man the bar for a while

as I train my newest employee. I'm going to have longer hours while I keep up with all the office duties as well, but I'm hoping it'll be a quick and easy transition.

Tammy eases up to the counter and places her tray on top. "What time is my new co-worker showing up?"

I glance at the clock behind me. "Probably in the next few minutes. I told her to be here by six so I could get her started before we get busy." Leaning onto my elbow, I ask Tammy the same question I've tossed out a few times already. "Are you sure you don't want to bartend instead of waitress?"

Tammy holds up her hands and backs away, like the idea of being behind a bar is repulsive. "Not a chance. I am too old to try and memorize recipes and lord knows I don't like people enough to have to stand here and listen to their sob stories."

"Are you sure?" I smirk at her. "You don't seem like the kind of woman who could pass up on all the juicy gossip."

"Juicy is one thing. Droning on and on about the same problems everybody else has irks me. Do you really think you want an irritated me trying to keep those customers happy?"

She makes sense. "Well played, Tammy. I will concede your point and leave you be."

"Thank you," she says with a quick nod. "Now if you don't mind, Jimmy would like an Old Fashioned and Dwayne has decided to upgrade to a Dos Equis instead of his usual Coors Light."

I snicker at her candor while I grab a fresh glass to make Jimmy's Old Fashioned. "Wow. Dwayne must be having a rough night."

"Like I said, droning on about the same old shit. Notice

I was able to happily walk away to talk to you instead."

"I get it." I pop the top on the beer bottle and hand the drinks over to her. "Here you go. Good luck getting in and out quickly and without rolling your eyes."

She walks away just as the door opens and a woman I assume is my newest bartender walks in. She looks vaguely familiar from the reception last week, but again, I wasn't paying much attention.

Now that I'm not busy and she's looking around the room, I can take a small amount of time to really look at her. She's beautiful. Dark hair falls down to the middle of her back. Long, lithe body with what appears to be even longer legs. Her body type alone means all the dancing jobs on her application make complete sense. It also has me wondering why she wants to work at a place like this.

I already know the answer. She told me on the phone—she needs the job. I'm just unclear why she's not still in her previous line of work. Her entire employment history was in Houston, so I assume she moved to the San Antonio area recently. Still, that doesn't answer all the questions running through my brain.

And I have a ton. Why did she move here? Does she like the area? Is she single?

Her assessment complete, she turns, her eyes finding mine, and smiles. I swear it hits me straight in the gut.

This is going to be a problem.

I'm already at half-mast in my pants and we've barely met. Nope. Can't happen. Not only am I at least a decade older than her, but I also need to keep my head down and remember that I'm the boss. Always. I will not fraternize with the staff and set that kind of example. I want this to be a classy place and getting a reputation for sleeping with my employees isn't the way to do that. This place will not fail because I can't keep it in my pants.

Still, as she practically glides up to the counter, I recognize this is going to take some very strong willpower on my part to hold these self-imposed boundaries.

"You're Paul, right?"

"I am." I do my best to act normal, despite my heart beating rapidly as she stands there, waiting for further instructions. I put out my hand and the moment our palms touch, it's like a current of electricity runs right through me. I'm stronger than this. I will not let some primal urge I learned how to control in high school derail my business practices. "It's nice to officially meet you, Kiersten."

"Likewise. And thanks again. I'm looking forward to getting started."

I grab a few papers from behind the bar and pass them to her. "I know we talked about the bartending job and I still plan for that to be your main function, but I realize we may need to have you do a couple of days of waitressing when Tammy is off. I hope that's not a dealbreaker. The pay is still the same so no worries about that."

She shrugs nonchalantly. "I don't mind. I actually thought about that on my way here. Tammy had told me it was only the three of you. It makes sense we all probably need to do double-duty sometimes."

Thirty seconds on the job, and I can already tell I'm not going to have to worry about having a disgruntled employee. Maybe I need to look at putting Tammy in charge of all the hiring. I almost laugh to myself at the thought. I'm sure she'd turn me down at having to interview potential candidates. Not that there's much need to beef up staff at this point. We need customers first.

I don't say any of that. Instead, I stick to the topic at hand. "I appreciate you being a team player while we get off the ground. First things first, let me get you a pen." I quickly find one sitting on the register and hand it to her. "There's a bunch of new hire paperwork to fill out, but once it's done, we'll get your account set up to clock in and get going."

"Sounds good to me."

Kiersten settles onto a stool and dives into the paperwork.

I keep busy by doing some quick inventory and keeping the Dos Equis and Old Fashioneds coming. An older couple sits close together at a table in the corner, quietly chatting, their hands constantly touching each other. A new guy I haven't seen here before laughs loudly across the room as he battles it out with Dwayne at the dartboard. Tammy hustles about, seeming pleased that Kiersten is here and not just because she already likes her better than she ever did Desiree. I pretend not to notice every time she looks at the newest employee and then winks at me, but I see it. Acknowledging her attempts at matchmaking is the last thing I need.

However, ignoring Tammy doesn't mean I'm not sneaking glances at Kiersten, observing small things about her, like the crinkle between her eyebrows when she concentrates and the way she taps the top of the pen on her chin as she reads the questions. All things I shouldn't be noticing but do because I apparently have no willpower.

The other thing I realize is that she looks familiar. And not just because of the reception. After driving myself crazy searching my memory for where I've seen her before, I finally give up and go a different route.

"Can I ask you a question?"

Kiersten looks up, a small smile on her lips. "Sure."

"Why do I know you?"

Her brows furrow. "What?"

"I feel like I've met you before or we've interacted. I just can't put a finger on it."

She looks off like she's searching her own memories for the answer. "Oh man, it could be anything. I used to come visit my best friend when she went to Southeast. We never came here, but we frequented a few different bars. Could that be it?"

"Maybe. Who's your friend?"

"Lauren Bagley."

I shake my head slightly. The name doesn't ring a bell.

"Oh." She snaps her fingers like she's figured it out. "It's probably from Annika."

"Jaxon's wife?"

"Yeah. After the… um… incident…" her face falls, as does mine I'm sure. "…we would only go to the place Jaxon's old boss worked at. That was you right? Jaxon's boss?"

It was. He and I didn't work together very long. The *incident* she's referring to is Jaxon interrupting as a guy drugged and raped Annika behind the dumpster of Ambrosia where we were both working at the time. It was a few years ago, but it's not something I've ever forgotten. It's actually why I left Ambrosia and moved on to a quieter scene. I wanted to get away from the constant memories and the fear of it happening to someone else on my watch. It wasn't my fault, per se. But that doesn't stop the guilt and wondering if I could have done something to prevent it.

My job change worked to all our benefit, though. Jaxon and I stayed in touch and as Annika started venturing out more, she was most comfortable hanging out at places where I worked. She didn't need to explain why she would only drink bottled water that she opened herself, and I made sure to keep a close eye on her and her friends. I was never actually a bouncer but after witnessing something like that, being protective came naturally.

As vague memories of Annika sitting around at my former place of employment, more interested in the football games on the televisions behind the bar, than partying, I nod.

"That has to be it. Annika would come with her roommate and another friend."

Kiersten nods vigorously. "That was us. Lauren was the roommate and I was the other friend. You probably don't remember us because we were the ones on the dance floor the whole time."

Now that we've figured it out, I do suddenly remember Kiersten catching my eye before. She would rarely stop moving to grab a drink, too interested in dancing. I remember thinking she was stunning on the dance floor—graceful and sensual. She knew how to move her body in ways no one else even came close to.

"Wasn't there another person? All I remember is she was really short and had a really short boyfriend."

Kiersten laughs. It's boisterous and fun, the kind of sound we need around here. "Yes! What was her name." She snaps her fingers a few times. "Um… Ellery! She was a gymnast as was her boyfriend."

"That explains the height."

"I think Lauren still sees her on social media but she sort of disappeared after graduation. Moved off with her boyfriend or something."

I'm glad to figure out our connection so it stops making me insane, but realizing my attraction actually started a long time ago isn't going to make it any easier to hold to my boundaries.

"Well," I finally say trying to hold my resolve, "I'm glad Annika and Jaxon have such good friends."

"Oh, trust me. I'm the one who is grateful for them." Shifting gears, she picks up the papers in front of her and taps them on the counter, making sure they're put together evenly. "I think these are done. What now boss?" she asks playfully as she hands them over.

Damn, she's cute. This is going to be rough.

Nope. Not going there. I will not allow any distractions to my business. Failure isn't an option.

"First things first. How are your mixed drink recipes?"

"Depends on the drink. I know some of the basics—Bloody Mary, martinis, margarita, things like that. The less common ones I probably need to learn."

"That's all you need to get started. Let me show you the office where you can leave your stuff and we'll get you all set up."

She flashes me that smile again before hopping off the stool and following me to the back. I just shake my head. Hiring her was a great idea. I just hope I don't screw up all my other ideas because of it.

EIGHT

Kiersten

Working at Frui Vita is turning out better than I expected. It's not teaching dance, which I miss desperately, but I enjoy the work I'm doing, and learning recipes for mixed drinks hasn't been that hard. Not that we have that many specialty drinks orders. But it's kind of fun coming in a little early and creating something new every day. It's only for Paul to taste test so he knows I'm making progress in my training, but considering he's trusting me behind the bar alone more, it's nice to have the feedback.

It also means I get to spend some alone time with him. I shouldn't be nearly as happy about that part as I am. But god he smells good. And his unruly brown hair that always looks like he's been thoroughly fucked, which of course gives me images of what I imagine he looks like naked. And every time he talks his voice makes me want to melt into a puddle.

Oh boy. I should not have a crush on my boss. Shouldn't, but do.

Even now as I take a free minute to load the dirty glasses into the dishwasher rack, I'm thinking about his broad chest and how it gives me the feeling there is some raw power behind his calm demeanor. It's not just his physique though. We also have interesting conversations in between customers and share laughs regularly. Altogether, it's a recipe for my hormones to flare every time we work together. This is why my new routine on the drive over every night is to chant "he's my boss and off-limits. He's my boss and off-limits," hoping it'll sink it. It never does.

I will admit, however, my job is more pleasant because we all get along well. Whether it's Paul or even Tammy, I really do enjoy being here. It's not a dance studio, but it's a great consolation job.

The only downside is working nights. I'm not a night owl by nature, and it only gives me half days with my baby. Speaking of, I take advantage of the few minutes of downtime I have to wipe my hands off and grab my phone, pulling up the video Lauren sent me earlier. In it, Carson and Heath are standing in front of the television dancing to The Incredibles theme song and pretending to be super heroes. Health grabs my boy and takes off around the room, making Carson fly while he giggles and squeals. I slump against the counter as I watch, happy he's having a good time, but also sad I'm no there to see it in person.

I take a deep breath to center myself. Yes, it sucks that I'm not with him but I recognize two important things— most single moms have less time than I do with their kids, and most single moms don't have a pseudo-family to lean on when necessary. I know Carson is in the best hands when I'm gone even if it's tough on me.

Getting back to work, I take a moment to rinse out the shaker from my last batch of martinis, and I barely hear the door open until someone calls out.

"Hey, bartender!" Lauren yells and my stomach immediately jumps with excitement. Having spent the last few minutes thinking of the love of my life, and knowing Lauren is with him tonight has me automatically assuming my pudgy baby is probably running in with her looking for me. When I don't hear him, I deflate just a little, but quickly finish what I'm doing. My best friend is still here, after all.

"Where's my boy?" I inquire as she eases up to the bar.

"He is still at the house with Uncle Heath. They are on hour two of reading all the books."

I pop open a new pale ale I want her to try and hand it over. "You're exaggerating."

"Nope. Remember how I told you Uncle Heath wants Carson to feel at home with us?"

"Oh, god. What did he do?"

"Three words… Barnes. And. Noble."

I groan. "You really need to give that man some offspring."

"Hell no. The minute I pop out a baby, my gymnastics days are over. Unless Depends comes out with a brand of leotards which I am uninterested in trying out, I'm good letting Heath dote on your kid for a long, long time." She takes a sip of the drink. "What is this anyway?"

"It's an apple pie pale ale. Something new Paul wanted us to try out and see what customers think before stocking it for the fall." I raise my eyebrows in question as she tries it a second time.

She licks her lips before giving me her opinion. "I like it. I'm not a huge ale drinker but this is something I could go for."

"Good to know." I toss the bottle cap in the trash.

"We've tried it with a couple of our regulars who gave two thumbs up, but they've all been older men. I'll let Paul know the female demographic approves as well."

Glancing around, I quickly make sure everyone's glasses are still full before leaning against the bar and taking a breather.

"What brings you out tonight anyway? I expected you to be on viewing number six hundred of The Incredibles tonight."

Lauren groans. "I love your son but I'm really sick of that movie. It's wildly unfair that Elastagirl has mom hips and still looks fantastic in her costume."

"Maybe because she's a cartoon."

"I don't care. Disney needs to think about the kind of image they're portraying for the women out there. It's depressing."

I snicker. She's ridiculous sometimes. "Leotard envy is what drove you out tonight, huh?"

She takes an even longer swing and drops her bottle on the counter. "Actually, Annika called me. She wants to get out of the house. I guess Jaxon is doing a volunteer clinical tonight and she didn't feel like being home by herself."

"That's unlike her. Married life must be making her needy if she wants to go to a bar."

This time Lauren laughs. "Maybe. Secretly I think she just wants to show off the pictures from her honeymoon and this is a good way to catch us both at the same time."

"Don't sound annoyed with it. You know you're dying to see them."

Lauren sighs loudly and drops her chin onto her hand. "You're not wrong. I'm just so damn happy for them. They give me hope."

A loud *thunk* reverberates through the room. Looks

like Dwayne found the new dartboard Paul had installed.

"What kind of hope do you need? You're living with your professional football player boyfriend in his giant house. If anyone should be looking for inspiration in the relationships around here, it should be me."

Lauren pulls her bottle to her lips but peeks up through her eyelashes at me, batting them just slightly. It's a clear sign I'm not going to like what she has to say next.

"I'm pretty sure Paul's single."

I shake my head. I was hoping she wouldn't go there but I knew that was coming eventually. "I will admit he's nice to look at and a really great guy. Plus, he's a little older and that maturity is damn attractive… "Shaking my head, I pull myself out of the rabbit hole I'm falling in and refocus. "But he's also my boss which makes him a no-go."

Lauren gestures with her hand like my boundary is ir-relevant. "Who cares? You're both adults and it's not like Tammy is single. There's no competition."

Speaking of my co-worker, she makes her way over just as her name is said.

"Why am I no competition? What are we competing about anyway? It's not that damn dartboard, is it? I swear I'm gonna get nailed in the head one of these days."

"I hope not. I don't do blood well," I say, making sure to quickly move to another topic. "Does Dwayne need an-other?"

"Nope," Tammy replies and I'm hopeful she forgot the original question. "Says he doesn't need his beer to taste all fruity. Wants to go back to Dos Equis."

Amused, I grab a bottle from the small fridge and pop the top. "Well, I appreciate his attempt at trying to be re-fined through drink, even if it didn't last long."

Tammy huffs a laugh. "Yeah, that's what it is. An attempt at being sophisticated. It has nothing to do with the alcohol content."

"It has the same percent as Coors Light."

Tammy holds up her hand to stop me. "I know that honey. He just doesn't seem to and I'm not correcting him. The last thing he needs is anything over four-point-two proof. Now," she turns to Lauren, "What am I apparently competing for and what is the prize?"

I groan. I was hoping we moved past this. Lauren, on the other hand, is delighted.

Leaning in like she's telling Tammy a secret she says, "Paul. He's single, right?"

A look of understanding crosses Tammy's face. "Ah yes. That man is a tall drink of man-candy for sure."

I burst out laughing at her candor while Lauren exclaims, "That's what I said. But she won't go for it."

"I am not sleeping with my boss, Lauren. It's in bad taste."

Lauren drops her chin to her chest grumbling, "She's such a buzzkill." Tammy, on the other hand, doesn't ever mince words. Not even now.

"Listen, honey, there are only three of us here and my man has no reason to worry about me straying so I'm not going to make a drama out of you banging the boss behind closed doors." Lauren gestures her hand in an "I told you so" fashion, but Tammy's not done. "Unless you do it in the office when I'm trying to get my stuff, I'm the last person who will raise a stink about some good old fashion lovemaking."

Lauren can't help it. She starts giggling. I need to double-check the alcohol content on this apple pie. Giggles mean it's already going to her head.

"Besides," Tammy continues. "That tight little twenties body isn't going to last forever. You better get your kicks while you can. Take it from someone who made sure she'd have lots of memories to last a lifetime."

I shake my head at her and then gesture my understanding as Dwayne holds his beer up and waves it at me.

"I will take that under advisement. But Dwayne is getting antsy over there so maybe we can table this conversation."

Tammy rolls her eyes. "It's a wonder that man can keep his electricity on with how much he spends every night."

"He's just lonely," I argue. "He's not doing any harm."

"Yet. Like I said," she says as she picks up the bottle. "One of these days a dart is gonna get me right in the noggin. Mark my words."

She walks away, making quick work of delivering Dwayne's drink and bussing the recently vacated tables.

"I like her." Lauren slaps her hand on the counter.

My eyes widen in amusement. "Okay, drunky." I slowly pull the beer away from her. "No more ale for you tonight."

"Oh stop. I'm not drunk." She snatches the bottle back. "I just really want you to get laid. I think Tammy does, too."

"As much as I appreciate that, the last time I was laid, I ended up a single mom. It's probably best not to tempt fate that way. Want something else?"

"Yeah. Give me another one of those apple pie things. Also, it's sad you haven't had sex in over three years."

She shudders which elicits a laugh from me.

"And you're ridiculous," she continues. "Just because you got pregnant one time doesn't mean it'll happen again."

"No, it doesn't." I pop the top off another bottle and

hand it to her, leaning on the counter. "But we both know how that ended and I think it's best if I avoid flippant relationships."

Her eyes darken as we both remember the shit show Spence put me through, even after he died. I quickly push it out of my mind. I don't want to think about it. It's over. I will never go through that again. And I'll be damned if I put my son through it.

"Fine," she finally concedes. "You win. This time. But I'm not going to give up on helping you find a man. You deserve some happiness.

"I have happiness. His name is Carson and he's almost three years old. He has a fantastic Aunt Lauren and an even better Uncle Heath."

"Hey!" she protests playfully. I ignore her.

"And as much as I love that he has them, I just hope they all don't become so attached that he gets hurt when they do finally have kids."

She shakes her head and swallows her drink that seems to have gotten stuck in her throat temporarily. "Not gonna happen. My man doesn't love just anyone. But once he decides you're part of his inner circle, you're in for life. And Carson is basically his whole circle these days. That's what happens when a grown man who is still a boy at heart has too much money and finds someone he can buy toys for, which is really just him justifying buying toys."

I laugh out loud and grab a glass, filling it with ice and some Dr. Pepper to give me a shot of caffeine. "Is that what it is?"

"Absolutely. I'm not sure which one of them is more spoiled. Heath is already planning Carson's birthday party."

My jaw drops in shock. "Are you kidding me?"

"Nope. I hope that doesn't bother you."

"It doesn't," I say with a laugh. "You know I'm the worst party planner."

"Which is why I didn't hire you to plan my wedding," an unexpected voice says.

"Annika!" Lauren gives her a tight hug, as surprised as I am that we didn't see her come in. "You look fantastic. Very tan and rested."

I nod in agreement. Honeymooning looks good on her.

"Thanks," Annika says sheepishly and turns to me. "Hi, Kiersten. Can I get my usual?"

"One unopened bottle of water, coming right up."

As suspected, Annika opens her phone and holds up a picture of her lounging in a cabana, white sand and crystal blue water in the background.

Lauren snatches the phone from her and gasps at the photo. "Annika, this is beautiful. And damn girl. Look at you being all super-model like with your sexy one-piece and floppy hat. I didn't even know you owned a floppy hat."

"It was an impulse buy in the airport," she explains while surveying over Lauren's shoulder as she swipes through the pics. She absentmindedly plays with the label on her water bottle as she tells us all about their honeymoon and everything they did. From what I'm gathering, it was a whole lot more of what we saw in that picture—mostly lounging around in a cabana with a couple of tours through the rainforests. It sounds heavenly and I can't help but wonder if I'll ever be as happy and in love as she is. I ignore the small pang of jealousy as I watch my two best girlfriends chat about their lives, each as one part of a happy couple.

Instead, I do my best to focus on the important parts. I

have a good job, a great son, and friends who seek me out at my place of employment so I can at least be part of the conversation, even if it's in between customers. It isn't a girl's night, but things could be worse than making money while chatting with my friends.

NINE
Paul

Looking around the room, I try to envision the changes I want to make to this place. Obviously, we need a few upgrades and a solid coat of paint. Past that, I'm still kind of stumped.

The biggest and most pressing issue is what to do about the stage. Do I keep it or get rid of it? I've never actually seen live music in this place, not even before I took over, and I'm not sure where I would begin if I decided to make that happen. Do I even want to open that can of worms? It sounds like a lot of coordination and one more project for me to have to tackle. I don't know if I have it in me at this point. The only thing I do know is I need to make some changes pretty soon.

Kiersten walks up. I don't have to see her to know. I can smell her shampoo before I see her. Damn she smells good. "Hey, boss. Whatcha doing?"

It's just us tonight. Tammy is taking advantage of the fact that both she and her husband are off and have a date night planned. She's been talking about it non-stop for the last couple of days. I'm glad the timing worked out for them.

I'm also glad she isn't here to interrupt my thoughts. I've talked about renovations before but Tammy always says the same thing—"Don't fix what ain't broke."

Unfortunately, I may be the one who's broke if I don't figure something out.

"Trying to decide what kind of vibe I want in here."

"Meaning?"

"The stage." I point at the offending area and let out a deep sigh.

"Ah." She crosses her arms and pops out her hip. I try hard not to notice how sexy the pose makes her look and keep myself focused on the task at hand. "The stage that's being used for storage."

I wish she were wrong, but she's not. It's sort of ended up being a "catch all" for oversized boxes and various equipment we don't need right now, but probably will. "Most of that stuff was cleared out of the apartment in the back. I meant to get rid of it..."

"But there are only so many hours in the day to get everything done."

"Yep. And I'm honestly not sure if we'll need any of it. Well, except for the obvious."

Placing her hands on her hips, Kiersten gets a determined look on her face. "Let's talk this out then. You've mentioned renovations before. What do you want to do?"

That's the biggest question of them all. "I haven't really decided. I'd like to cater to a more upscale clientele than we've got now."

Kiersten pokes my arm playfully. "Dwayne isn't high end enough for you?"

I can't help it, I laugh. She puts me at ease in a way no

one else does. Even just talking through my thoughts so I can process them is much more helpful than she knows.

"Dwayne is like the mascot. He's not going anywhere."

"You cemented that fact when you put up that dartboard," she banters. This is what it's always like between us—easy conversation and smart quips. I enjoy working with her more than I should.

I enjoy jacking off to thoughts of her more than I should, too. That is a secret that will go with me to the grave.

I run my hand down my face and chuckle. "I did, didn't I? At least I know we'll have one regular customer. If I can't figure out a way to bring a new demographic in here, I may as well leave things as they are. Ideally, I'd like to cater to the sports teams in the area. Jaxon mentioned liking that we're kind of a hole-in-the-wall type place where he didn't have to worry about football fans or reporters. That's why they chose it for the reception. It got me thinking that something like that could be an option."

"That is a great idea," she says with no hesitation whatsoever.

"I thought so. If I can figure out how to market to the sports teams in the area. And get this place up to snuff. No use spending the money if we don't get anything out of it."

Kiersten scoffs. "That is a terrible thing to say. Do you want to know what I think? What changes could be made to bring in that demographic?"

"Yes, please." I really mean it. Maybe her perspective will help fix my own. A decorator I am not.

"Follow me," she says with a wave of her hand.

Like the good boy I am, I do.

"This right here." Kiersten pats her hand on the railing that encloses the dance floor. "What is the purpose of this?"

"I have no idea. Although most people use it to lean on while they watch others dance. I suppose it's nice that it's wide enough to set down your drink."

Kiersten purses her lips. "Well, that's the biggest load of horse shit I've ever heard."

I bark out a laugh. "What do you mean?"

"Exactly how many times have you seen people dance in here?"

"You did the other night."

A blush creeps up her face. When things are slow, which is almost always, she takes a minute to go shimmy on the dance floor. The few regular patrons we have seem to love when she makes them partner up with her. While I'm glad they're happy, part of me hates it. Kiersten just comes alive on that dance floor, her smile and laughter uncontrollable from exhilaration. Whenever she dances, everyone around her stops what they're doing to watch her and I find myself irritated. I want to be the only one dancing with her, the only one watching her move to the music. But instead, I have to contain myself behind the bar watching with everyone else.

Kiersten licks her lips and clears her throat. "Well, yes. Besides then. When is anyone other than me dancing?"

"The reception is the only time I can think of."

"Exactly," she says like it's the obvious answer. Which it is but I'm not sure what she's getting at quite yet. "You say you want this place to be more of a premier bar, but it's got this funky, old-school country-western vibe to it. Like this should be a dance hall and have live music every night for a bunch of seventy-year-olds to hang out."

"Yeah, that's not what I'm going for. What do you suggest?"

"First things first." Her eyes brighten as she looks around the room and I can practically see the ideas as they hit her. I'm not sure which is more interesting—hearing what she has to say or watching her in her element. "Take down the railing. There's no reason for it and it's ugly. Once it's gone, we can fill in all this space with more tables and chairs, kind of make everything spread out a little bit. Maybe get some new, updated furniture."

Kiersten walks toward the stage and begins inspecting it. "Is this even the original design? It looks like it was extended at some point."

Looking at where she's pointing, I see exactly what she means. The joints don't fit together quite right and the wear on the different parts is significantly different.

"You're right. Think we should go back to the old design?"

She nods and keeps canvassing the area, probably trying to figure out where the original structure is. "I do. If I'm seeing it right, it'll cut the stage in half which gives even more room. You can even add a pool table over here."

I chuckle. "Do you want Dwayne to ever go home? He'll never leave if we get a pool table."

She smiles at me and it hits me right in the gut. I love how carefree and lively she is. Kiersten is always this way at work. It makes me wonder if she's this happy-go-lucky in her home life, too. Not that I'll ever find out. Still, I can't help my own curiosity.

"We'll just put a bow on it and tell him it's our gift to him for being such a good customer," she says with a laugh. "But seriously. I don't know if the last owner was planning to have lots of live music or concerts or something, but this area is wasted space we could be taking advantage of. We could keep the original design for things like karaoke night or, oh! Trivia night. That's always fun. Interesting things to get people engaged and draw a crowd. Have five-dollar buckets of beer on those nights and do some easy marketing on social media. This place will be hopping in no time."

"What about the dance floor?"

"With all the extra space, we can move it over, add tables around it, and voilà. A whole new feel."

Looking around, I rub my bottom lip absentmindedly trying to envision all the ideas she has. My imagination can't necessarily see it, but even from a logical standpoint, everything she's suggesting makes sense.

"That sounds feasible actually. And with the exception of labor and some supplies, it may not cost much."

"And," she adds excitedly, "it'll probably only take a day or two to pull off which means not closing the bar for very long."

"Not a bad idea. Just need to hire some labor and go check the home improvement store for a price list." I run my hand down my face, already tired from being here so much. Having Kiersten means I'm not always at the front, but living on the property means I can't get away from my job either. I'm not complaining. It's just the reality of being a business owner.

"Are you okay?"

I look over at her, confused by her question and the concern in her eyes. "What? Oh yeah. Just tired. I feel like I work non-stop."

"You do. You need some time for your brain to rest."

I scoff. "No, I need my brain to work faster to figure out some solutions so I can take some real time off."

Kiersten purses her lips. I know that look. It's the same one my dad used to give me when I would say something he not only didn't agree with, but thought was ridiculous. It wouldn't end there. "The look" was a precursor to him being in my face, spewing shit about what a loser I was and how I'd never amount to anything. Of course, he didn't stick around long enough to see if he was right or not. Douchebag.

I push thoughts of my asshole dad out of my mind, knowing Kiersten's expression isn't actually the same, just triggered an unwelcome memory. "Your brain won't do that if it doesn't have some downtime. I don't mean sleeping. I mean a full mental break. Why don't you get out of here for a while? Come with me to a barbecue tomorrow."

My eyebrows lift slightly at the offer. I know it's not a date, but it's still an extended invitation to spend time together outside of work. Part of me wants to say yes immediately. The other part knows agreeing would be testing my own boundaries. "I appreciate that, but I can't just show up at someone's house uninvited."

"It's not uninvited. I'm inviting you," she argues. "And It's not a random person's house. It's Jaxon Hart's best friend's house."

I think back through my memories quickly. "Do I know his best friend?"

"I don't know. Do you follow the San Antonio Steer?"

"As much as anyone else in town." Which is a lot. Every football fan follows the hometown team. It's like a requirement to live in Texas.

"Then you probably do know Heath Germaine."

"Oh, yeah. I do know him. Did he come to the reception?"

Kiersten laughs and we head back over to the bar as we wait for the first customers to arrive. "How could you miss him? He was the best man and he's huge."

"I was a little too enamored by Jaxon's dad. The man is a legend and he was in *my bar*. I almost got teary."

Kiersten rolls her eyes playful and ties her apron around her waist since she waitressing tonight. "You men are all alike with that hero-worship crap. But if it helps, Jason Hart will be at the barbecue tomorrow. Does that give you an incentive to go?"

Honestly, yes. But it still feels weird to show up at some pro ball player's humble abode—two degrees of separation or not.

"Kiersten, I can't just show up at Heath Germaine's house for a barbecue." I grab a couple of limes out of the fridge and prepare to slice them. Kiersten grabs the lemons to do the same while she keeps trying to pressure me.

"Yes, you can. He's my friend, too. Look, I'll text him right now." She pulls her phone out of her back pocket and relays what she's typing. "Can. I. Bring. A. Friend. To. The. Barbecue?"

Just a few seconds later, the phone chimes. She looks at it and smiles, turning it around to show me.

It reads, "Of course. The more the merrier."

I could keep arguing but in truth, I do need to get out of this place for a few hours to decompress. And in general, I'm curious to see what kind of home a pro athlete with a multi-million-dollar contract lives in. I keep that bit to myself, though.

"Fine. I'll go. But only so I can be somewhere other than Walmart for food. And to catch up with Jaxon for a bit."

They aren't total lies. I just keep the part about seeing what Kiersten's like outside of work to myself.

I sigh at how pathetic I am. She didn't even ask me on a date and I've already caved.

TEN

Kiersten

"I do it, mama! I do it!" Carson is practically hysterical as he jumps up and down, making sure I don't accidentally ring the doorbell. Pressing buttons is his newest favorite thing. Riding on an elevator with him is an adventure because you never know how many floors you're going to visit when his sneaky little fingers start lighting things up.

Thankfully there's only one at Heath and Lauren's monstrosity of a house, unless you count the buttons on the gate code. Fortunately, Carson couldn't reach those from his car seat and had no choice but to let me do it or we'd still be stuck outside. This time, though, he won't give me any grace.

"I do it!" He yells one last time before I pick him up and balance him on my hip.

"I know, I know. Here ya go."

Leaning forward, he stretches out his little finger to accomplish his goal. You would think he just won the lottery with how delighted he is at ringing a doorbell.

It takes a few seconds until Lauren's voice comes through the speaker.

"Hang on, I'm coming."

I try to wait patiently while the pint-sized holy terror runs in circles around my legs. He loves coming here. It's literally his home away from home. I just hope he doesn't get too used to living the posh life. It is highly unlikely I'll ever come into enough money for something like this.

Don't misunderstand, I get their need for a home in a gated community complete with several forms of security. His job practically demands it. But life would be easier for all of us if I could just let myself in like Lauren does at my small apartment.

The door finally flies open and my best friend stands there with a huge smile on her face, an even bigger margarita in her hand. "Carson!" she yells and picks up the wiggling toddler to kiss all over his face.

"Yep. That's how it works. I'm irrelevant now," I grumble with no actual malice. This is the way it should be.

"If you were cute and tiny I'd snuggle you too." Lauren lets Carson go and shouts, "Uncle Heath is in the back yard!" as he runs away.

"Please don't snuggle me. That would just be weird."

"Which is why it's good you're not cute and tiny. Come on." She gestures for me to follow her. "Party's out back."

We walk through the immaculate living room and pass an even more immaculate kitchen. If I was a chef, I'd never leave that room. I may not be much of a cook but even I recognize an industrial-grade, six-burner gas stove is something to covet. Good thing I'm more the lounge around type. The almost floor to ceiling glass doors leading out to the patio are wide open revealing the stunning backyard set up that is my favorite part of their home.

The large covered patio has an amazing outdoor kitchen on the right. Next to it is a beautiful table that could seat at least twelve people. The rest of the space is dedicated to relaxation with cushion covered lounge chairs, a couple of hammocks, and of course a giant TV for watching whatever sport is on. Looks like today Lauren got her way since it's a replay of the NCAA college gymnastics championship meet.

Beyond that, the oversized lap pool is surrounded by a wrought-iron gate to keep rambunctious kids out. Any given day the term "rambunctious kid" might be referring to one of my adult friends, but today it's just poor Carson who is staring through the spindles hoping one of us will have pity on him and let him in the water.

Sorry kid. You'll have to ask Uncle Heath later.

Speaking of, Heath is busy manning the grill as he chats with some of his teammates and their significant others. Or at least I assume those are his teammates based on their physique and Steers logoed wardrobes.

"Hey Heath," I say and wave to his friends as I approach.

They all greet me kindly, including Heath. His eyes light up and he pulls away from the food long enough to give me a hug. "Hey girl! Where's my little man?"

Heath and I have come a long way from when we first met. Back when he and Lauren started dating, she was injured and kind of a mess because of missing an entire season of competition. I jumped in to help her, like I have since we were teenagers, and Heath hated it. It was as if he didn't understand who I thought I was barging my way into his territory when he had it all under control.

That may be an over-exaggerated version of the beginnings of our relationship, but it's pretty accurate from my perspective. Little did I know that he was actually in love with Lauren and feeling wildly protective due to his own issues. Once I figured that out, I backed off a bit and let him take care of my best friend.

It was around this time when I found out I was pregnant with Carson. Things were starting to smooth over as Heath and I got to know each other. But then Spence died, and my entire life went into a tailspin. Lauren immediately jumped in to help me, again, like we always have since high school, and that's when Heath suddenly figured out that she and I were not just friends. We're more like family. In Heath's mind, that means we were all family together.

We've been friends ever since. I'm never quite sure if he likes me or just my kid, but that part doesn't bother me at all. As long as you are good to my child, I don't mind being part of the package deal. Besides, the real winner here is Carson and for that, I will always be grateful to Heath.

"He has his poor little face smooshed up to the gate, staring at the pool." I pout my lips, over-exaggerating how sad the moment is.

Heath laughs lightly and looks over my shoulder. "Aw. That breaks my heart. I think his Uncle Heath needs to help him out. Lauren, where's the sunscreen?"

She looks up from the conversation she's having and furrows her brow at him. "Um, since when are you worried about getting tan lines?"

"Since Carson needed to go swimming and his little white baby skin isn't as durable as mine against sunburns."

She points at him in understanding. "That makes more sense. I'll grab it. It's in the laundry room."

I shake my head at the pair of them. "Of course, you have sunscreen for him. It's the gentle for baby kind, too, isn't it?"

"You know it. I got a value pack on sale at Costco. I'm ready for him and all the other kids you have."

I swat at him playfully. "You shut your face with that delusional talk. One is enough for this single mom, thank you very much. I'm already worn out."

"This is why I like to take my little man outside in the afternoons and do manly things like mow the lawn and pull weeds. Gets that energy out and teaches him important life skills."

I hold up my hand as I have a lightbulb moment. "Hold on. Are you the one who taught my kid it's okay to pee in the grass?"

Heath's expression turns sheepish as his friends snicker and chide him. "Uh, well ya see, we were doing some yard work and when you gotta go, you gotta go."

"Heath!" I exclaim. "He mooned the entire street in front of the daycare the other day when I dropped him off."

The other guys roar with laughter and at least one of the women I haven't met yet says, "Y'all all think it's funny until it's you the daycare director is side-eyeing."

I point at her with a, "Yes. Thank you," and turn back to my friend with a sigh. "I should have known who he got that from."

Heath shrugs a shoulder and flips some burners on the grill, probably to avoid looking at me. "It's a man thing. You ladies wouldn't understand."

I scoff at his excuse. "The next time I see you whip it out on the field because it's *a man thing* I might believe you."

"Uh… why is my boyfriend whipping things out in public? Do I wanna know?" Lauren asks as she saunters up to us, sunscreen in one hand and a drink for me in the other.

"Thanks." I take it and begin to sip. Mmm. Good.

Heath immediately snatches the sunscreen from her. "I'll take this. And I'll hand you this." He gives her the spatula. "And I'm going to see my way out of this awkward moment. I have some swimming to do." He quickly kisses Lauren on the cheek, then turns on his heel and yells, "Carson!" as he hurries away.

Lauren looks at me, confusion all over her face. "Why am I suddenly in charge of the food?"

"Your boyfriend got caught teaching my kid how to make bad choices."

She thinks for a second before saying, "Sounds about right. But that doesn't explain why I'm stuck cooking. I've never used a grill."

"I got it." One of Heath's teammates takes the spatula from her and begins manning the burgers and whatever other goodies Heath has tucked in the aluminum foil. This guy must have the same fear of Lauren burning the food like I do. Or burning down the house. It's too nice of a place to risk it.

She takes the next few minutes to introduce me to everyone. I was right—almost everyone is somehow affiliated with the Steer. They're all friendly enough, but we don't really have much in common and as sometimes happen at events like this, the conversations eventually taper off between groups of friends.

I end up settling into one of the lounge chairs, while Lauren answers the door again, and watch as the two men in my life finally make it through the gate and climb in the water. A couple of other guys join them and before long, they're tossing Carson back and forth making him squeal with delight. I'm surprised they can catch him with how much sunscreen Heath slathered on Carson's little body. No wonder Heath bought the value pack.

"For having a single mom and no dad, that kid sure has more male interaction," Lauren declares as she sits next to me, her thoughts mirroring my own.

"Seriously. I can't tell if it's because he's just so darn cute that people gravitate toward him or because Heath is the best."

"Probably a little bit of both."

"What's a little bit of both?"

We look up at Annika who must have just arrived, Jaxon heading off to say hi to some other guests.

"Hey." I scooch over a bit so she can squeeze in. "How are you always sneaking up on us?"

"Must be a gift. What's a little of both?"

I gesture out to the water. "We're just appreciating how Heath has taken over the role of father figure for Carson, and how my son doesn't lack for male attention at all because of it."

"They are really bonded," Annika remarks and we all laugh at the look on Carson's face when someone finally slips and he accidentally goes underwater after a particularly hard toss. It doesn't seem to faze him. Once he wipes the water from his eyes he starts yelling, "'gain! Do it 'gain!"

"That kid is a mess," Lauren says under her breath while we laugh.

"It's good he has so many uncles to wrestle around with. It releases chemicals in his brain that'll help make him smart." Leave it to Annika to know the medical benefits of throwing a toddler around a pool. She and Jaxon really are perfectly matched.

We sit in silence and watch for a while, enjoying the

calm of the day. I don't have to work, Carson is entertained, and food is on the way. Everything is nearly perfect. Except for one thing.

I glance down at my phone checking the time and to see if I have any missed texts. My face must give me away because Lauren nudges me.

"Where is Paul anyway? Did he text you?"

I groan. Of course, she would know that's who I was thinking about. She's never going to let this go. Maybe inviting him was a bad idea.

Annika leans forward so she can see both of us. "Paul from the bar? Is there something I don't know about?"

"No. There is nothing you need to know." There actually is. Namely the insanely strong feelings I have for my boss, but I will never admit it to these two.

"Kiersten has a crush on Paul," Lauren says immediately making me groan again. Now there are two of them. They're going to gang up on me, I just know it.

"I do not," I argue but I know the blush on my cheeks gives me away.

"You're turning awfully red for someone who is just friends with a hot guy." Lauren says it matter-of-factly and goes back to sipping on her margarita.

"It's summertime. I must have a sunburn on my cheeks." The argument falls flat even to my own ears.

"You're sitting in a covered patio."

"Et tu, Annika?"

"Yes. Yes Annika, too." Lauren slaps my thigh playfully. She's had enough to drink she's forgotten her own strength.

"Ow," I whine, rubbing my leg. "That actually hurt."

"No. What hurts is knowing that you're not being honest with yourself about how much you like him." She turns in her seat to stare me down. She's so close I have to lean back.

"I'm a little frightened of how aggressive you're being about this."

She huffs and sits back. "Kiersteeeeeeeeen." She draws out my name like this whole conversation is painful. It is, but not to her.

"Paul is my boss and he's at least a decade older than me. Can you please let this go? At least for today so you don't make work uncomfortable for me?" I plead. Lauren doesn't seem convinced, but Annika finally understands why I don't want to have this conversation now. Really, I don't want to have it ever, but I'll settle for this afternoon if it's all I can get.

"You're right." I knew Annika was my favorite. "We'll drop it while he's here. There's no reason to make him feel weird."

"Exactly."

"Especially since we don't know how he feels about you, yet," she tacks on.

"Wrong answer…"

Lauren's phone vibrates and she opens the screen to check her security app. "Well, we're about to find out because someone has finally arrived." She shakes the phone in my face, and I have to back away so it doesn't smack me in the nose.

"Okay, drunky. You just sit there, and I'll go answer the door."

I push out of the lounger and give them one last glare, gesturing to zip their lips, before heading back through the house to let Paul in. Fingers crossed my friends will keep their mouths shut. Honestly, with this group, you just never know.

ELEVEN
Paul

When Kiersten invited me to a barbecue, I wasn't expecting a house like this. Sure, it's in a gated community and the security is pretty unreal. Meaning, I didn't have a gate code so the armed guard, yes, *armed*, had to make sure my name was on some sort of list. That was kind of surprising.

What's surprising is how modest the house is in size. Don't get me wrong, it's huge by regular everyday standards. But it's not what I'd call a mansion either. Just really large. The landscaping is impeccable and I assume professionally maintained, if it weren't for the kid's plastic shovel in the mulch. I didn't realize Heath and Lauren had children. I must not have been paying as much attention to our local sports news as I thought.

It takes just a few minutes of waiting for the door to finally be answered by Kiersten, of all people.

"Hey," she greets with a bright smile. She's so damn beautiful I almost stumble over my own reply of "Hey." *Well done, Romeo.*

I quickly pull myself together by reminding myself of two undeniable truths. She's an employee and significantly younger than me. Would that make me a dirty old man?

It doesn't matter. Dating her is off-limits. Even if she is the first woman who has truly caught my eye in a very long time.

"Come on in." She steps aside for me to enter the house. "You got here just in time. Everyone's out back and the food is almost done. You hungry?"

"I could eat."

She smiles at me over her shoulder as she leads me through the house and the unintentional sexiness of the gesture hits me straight in the gut. I try to glance around as we walk through the living areas, but my eyes are too busy enjoying her backside. I really need to get laid. Having a crush on one of two employees isn't a good idea. I wish the angel on my shoulder would hurry up and shut down the devil on the other side. I'm getting tired of battling myself.

Stepping out through a set of sliding glass doors, Kiersten continues doing her best to make me feel welcome. "We've got mixed drinks in the blender out here and there's beer in the fridge. Or you can just have straight liquor. What do you prefer?"

"I'm good with beer."

"You got it."

She takes off into the outdoor kitchen area and I'm left standing alone, awed by the backyard. It's massive and perfect for entertaining. This one area is nicer than my entire business. It's got more people using it, too.

Shit.

I just realized I'm at a barbecue with a bunch of kids in their twenties. Maybe a few in their early thirties. For the most part, they're all babies. And yet they have more to show for it than I do. At least Heath Germaine does. But considering how many of the men here are obviously pro football players, it's a reasonable assumption that they all have some pretty nice digs.

That's not discouraging, per se. Just makes me all the more determined for my bar to succeed so I have something to show for myself.

I'm not left standing alone for long when a voice I recognize calls out.

"Hey Paul." Jaxon saunters over to greet me with a handshake and man hug.

"Good to see you, man. How was the honeymoon?"

Jaxon's eyes light up. "Amazing. St. Lucia was stunning. You ever been?"

"Nope." Kiersten hands me my beer with a smile and takes off to talk to her friends. "I'm sad to say I don't do much traveling."

"You should put it on your bucket list. It's fantastic."

Jaxon and I chat a bit more about his trip and the pediatric oncology specialty he's working toward. I never pegged the guy for a medical student when we worked together, but I'm glad he's found his calling. At some point into my second beer, Annika joins us, snuggling into her husband's side. When he kisses her on the forehead, I admit to wondering what it would feel like to have someone to be that comfortable with.

It's not that I haven't dated in the past. Hell, the thought of marriage has crossed my mind before, just in the very distant future. Still, I'm in my mid-thirties. Convention says I should have settled down long ago. I've never paid much attention to that thought process but seeing all these kids starting their lives makes me begin to wonder if I've been missing out.

"You know Lauren, right?" Jaxon asks as the tiny blonde bounces up to our group.

"Yeah, we've met a few times. Thanks for inviting me. Or letting Kiersten invite me," I clarify.

"The more the merrier," Lauren says and raises her glass, almost losing her balance. "Oh! Apparently, I've already had too much to drink."

I chuckle in response. "At least you're among friends. And no driving home for you."

"Right?" She gets an over-exaggerated happy expression, a clear indicator in my world of her lack of sobriety. "I should have parties more often."

"Maybe you should drink a little water so you don't get dehydrated." Annika hands Lauren a water bottle. She shrugs and begins chugging the whole thing without any resistance. I wish the drunks in my bar were always this compliant.

Jaxon just shakes his head, clearly amused by the antics. Somehow, I don't think this is the first time he's seen Lauren blitzed.

"And here's the man of the house," Jaxon announces. A very tall, very muscular Black man holding a toddler joins our group. "Paul, did you meet Heath at the reception?"

"I don't think I did." I hold my hand out to shake his. "Nice to meet you. You've got a great outdoor space here."

Heath looks around, admiring the area as he nods. "This is what sold me on the house. I didn't really care about the inside. That was all Lauren. But out here is my favorite space. I would be in that hammock over there all the time if I could be. Anyway, I'm glad you could make it. Kiersten says you've been working way too hard lately."

"She exaggerates. You know how it is when you're trying to get a business off the ground. It takes a while."

"It was a pretty cool place, though." Heath shifts the kiddo from one side to the other. The toddler doesn't stop rubbing his hands over the top of Heath's hair. He doesn't seem to notice. I'm not sure whose kid it is since they don't look alike at all. Unless maybe they adopted? But surely I would have heard about that. Regardless, they're obviously really close.

"You should swing by when you have a night off. It's pretty low-key. Not many customers yet so at least you won't get mobbed. First drink is on me."

Heath's eyebrows raise slightly. "Yeah, that sounds fun. We'll do that. Thanks, man."

"Of course. Any friend of Jaxon's and all that." Looking at the kiddo again, I can't stop myself from inquiring. "And who is this guy, huh?" I poke the kid's tummy because, well, I don't really know why. I guess that's what people do.

"This is Carson. Kiersten's boy but my little man, isn't that right?" Heath starts blowing raspberries on the boy's neck, making him squeal with delight, but I'm too stunned to really notice.

As if on cue, Kiersten walks up and wraps the tot in a towel.

"I cold, mama."

"I can see that," she replies with a laugh as she tucks the fabric around him. "Your lips are blue. You better tell Uncle Heath to turn the heater on in the pool."

His big brown eyes turn to the football player accusingly. "Turn on da heata, Unca Heat."

"Oh man, you're fine. You ain't no pansy. Tell your mama that. Say, I am no pansy."

I continue to watch the whole exchange, shocked by

this new information. Eventually, Heath recognizes Lauren is swaying, so he takes her hand and walks away to sit with some teammates. Carson goes with him, laying his head on Heath's massive shoulder. That's when I finally turn to Kiersten.

"You have a son?"

She cocks her head, likely feeling just as confused as I do. "You didn't know that?"

"No. We've worked together for almost two months and it never came up."

She looks off and thinks for a few seconds before answering. "Huh. That's weird because I know I've talked about him before. I think Tammy will kill me if I show her another cute baby picture."

Tammy knew and didn't tell me? That seems out of character for her. She made sure to tell me about Desiree's sugar daddy and when Dwayne's dog had gastrointestinal issues. Seems like Kiersten having a kid would have been the first thing she spilled.

I clear my throat at my spinning thoughts. I don't want to sound rude. "Well, he's really cute."

Kiersten bites her lip and smiles in his direction as he begins to entertain the crowd by demanding Heath become "a horsie, Unca Heat."

"He's the best thing I've ever done in my life," Kiersten says wistfully.

It shouldn't matter to me that she's a mom, and it doesn't in any important sense. But I hope this is the information I need to close the door on any potential relationship. Hell, I don't even know if Carson's dad is around. What I do know, however, is single moms have so much on their plates, the last thing she needs is me getting in the way, especially with her limited free time. And the last thing they both need is for me to fail them.

At least I have one more reason to stop pining over her. Maybe this is the reason that will finally stick.

93

TWELVE
Kiersten

"**I** need two fingers of whiskey for Jimmy, and I guess Dwayne has decided he likes what he calls *fruity drinks* after all, so if we have any more Apple Pie Ales, he'll take three."

Paul chuckles, the rumble in his chest lighting up my hormones. Lately, it's been my favorite sound and every night I find myself setting a goal to see how many times I can make it happen.

Damn Lauren for putting my crush into the forefront of my mind. I blame her for not being able to get him out of my thoughts since the other day at the barbecue. I refuse to believe it has anything to do with how much I enjoyed hanging out with him. Nope. It's all Lauren's fault.

"I knew he'd come around eventually. And he's in luck—I stocked up on some today." Paul pops the top off the bottle and puts it on the counter. "But he's only getting one at a time."

I shake my head in fake disappointment. "He's going to be really mad he has to stop playing darts to order another." Grabbing my tray, I drop the act and deliver the drinks as requested.

"Here ya go, gentlemen."

Dwayne looks over from the dartboard where he's getting ready for the next round of play by removing what Tammy and I refer to as *the weapons*. Let's face it—anything a drunk can throw in a bar fight doesn't have to be called by its official name. Darts are number one on that list. And Dwayne doesn't look happy already. "What is that? I ordered three."

"Sorry, Dwayne. Boss man says you can only have one at a time. But between you and me, they're best straight from the fridge anyway. The colder the better."

He considers my words then thanks me through his grumbles and gets back to his game. There is nothing Dwayne loves more than throwing pointy objects at that wall. Thank goodness he doesn't lose his aim the longer he drinks and isn't an angry drunk.

I quickly bus the vacated tables and wipe them down. There aren't many. It's another slow night. While it makes my job easier, I feel bad for Paul. I know he wants to increase business sooner rather than later, but it's slow going at this point. Sure, we're seeing a small increase in traffic, but I know it's nothing like he's hoping for.

Satisfied everything is covered for now, I head back to the bar to take a break and grab some caffeine.

Once I return the dirty glasses to the bar and load them into the dishwasher, Paul looks up from where he's counting bottles. He's holding an inventory form on a clipboard and I assume he's taking advantage of the lack of customers to get some extra tasks done.

He smiles at me and once again, my insides melt a little. "Taking a break?"

Grabbing a clean glass, I fill it with ice and flip on the soda gun. "I could use some caffeine to get me through the night."

"It's only nine. You hit a brick wall already?"

I shake my head and take a long drink. "Carson decided on the day he was born that he's a co-sleeper, but not even a snuggly one. He rolls around all night long. Last night was worse than normal. I don't know if he was having nightmares or what, but it makes for really bad sleep when you have a foot in your back."

"Oooh. And on your night off, too."

"Tell me about it." I fill the glass again, only sipping this time. "I should have known it would happen. Since I work nights, he only gets to sleep with me a couple of times a week now. I guess he's missing me or something. Maybe he's still transitioning a bit."

Paul tosses the clipboard aside and grabs his own clean glass. Only he fills his with water. "I was wondering about that. Where does he go when you're here?"

"You mean you couldn't tell at the barbecue? He stays with Lauren and Heath."

"Ah. That explains why Carson's comfortable with them. And by them, I mean Heath."

I giggle because he's not wrong. As much as Carson loves Lauren, he's all about Heath right now. "Oh yeah. They are basically best friends. And Heath just loves him so much. We argue all the time about how much he spoils my son."

Paul chuckles. "There are worse things, though, right?"

"Definitely." I lean back against the bar, taking some of the pressure off my feet. "They're the reason we moved here. Well, them and the Harts. The four of them are the best support system anyone could ask for."

Every once in a while, when I really think about it, I get almost teary with gratitude. Life is hard, but it would be much worse without them.

"I'm surprised his dad didn't put up a fight when you moved here. Or does he live in the area?"

I stiffen at the reminder. It's an innocent question and one I should have expected at some point, but it still catches me off guard. Spence's death is a topic I prefer not to think much about. Actually, Spence's life is not something I like to think about either. But I suppose there's no harm in telling Paul the truth. It's not like Spence is here to argue semantics. "Carson's dad died in a car accident a couple of months before he was born."

Paul's eyes soften and I know he thinks he struck a nerve. He did, but not in the way he thinks. "I'm sorry. That must have been tough. To lose him like that."

I shrug. I should feel sadness that Spence is gone, or at least sadness for my son who will never know his father. But after finding out things weren't what they seemed between us, and the shit show that followed for the three years after, I stopped being sad. As guilty as it makes me feel, which isn't much, I'm more relieved that Carson will never be raised in such a deceptive environment.

Crossing my arms, I carefully answer him. "Yes, but not really for the reasons you think."

"What does that mean?"

Sharing all my dirty laundry isn't high on my priority list, but something about Paul makes me feel safe. Like he won't judge me. Or maybe he will, but he still won't treat me any differently. Besides, Paul's been around for a long time. He knows the shit on everyone. Hell, he's a bartender by trade. I'm sure he's heard worse. Might as well lay it all out there.

Taking a deep breath, I begin the story. "He wasn't alone in the car."

"Was he with a friend or something?"

"He was with his fiancée."

I can tell by the look on Paul's face, he's deducing the wrong way regarding my involvement in the matter. While a false conclusion shouldn't matter, I don't want him making assumptions about me either. So, I clarify.

"A fiancée I didn't know he had."

Paul's face changes to a look of surprise, probably not unlike mine when I found out at his funeral that I wasn't his girlfriend. I was his side piece. An inconvenience his parents were trying to keep hidden and eventually rid themselves of. There's nothing like being escorted out of a funeral while you're seven months pregnant thanks to the deceased, to make it clear how absolutely unimportant you are.

"Her name was Blaire. She and I never crossed paths. We ran in different circles, so neither of us had any idea about the other. Or at least I assume she didn't know about me since she was radio silent about me being pregnant. It wasn't until Spence died, well *they* died, that I found out he had no intention of being with me."

"Wait… what? He didn't…"

I shake my head sadly. "Nope. Spence had been engaged to her for over a year, a match both sets of parents approved of long before they started dating. I guess it's a socialite thing or something. Because of the merger between two families and their corporations, me getting pregnant was a bigger problem than he let on. Apparently, he was stringing me along until he could figure out how to get rid of us. I didn't know any of this until I showed up at the funeral and was promptly confronted by his mother who was pissed."

"Hold on. She was mad the mother of her grandchild showed up at her son's funeral?"

I laugh humorlessly. "Mad is an understatement. She had security discreetly escort me out the back door, after she threatened to sue me for slander if I breathed a word of the pregnancy to the other family members. Said it was bad enough that Spence hadn't yet followed through on his promise to get rid of us."

"Holy shit. But you're sure he's the bad guy in this?"

"Positive. I ran into one of his "bros" out back. He had a lot of text exchanges to show me verifying everything she said." I sniff and look at the floor, holding my anger at bay. There's no reason to rile myself up again. It's over. Good riddance to all of them, even if I still kick myself for falling for his game. "I sure know how to pick 'em, right?"

Paul lets out a breath like he's not sure what the right answer is. "It sounds more like he was a master manipulator. I just can't wrap my brain around it. Like maybe his friend was wrong, too."

"Considering his family trip to the Bahamas was actually spent with her on a pre-wedding planning vacation a month before they died, I think it's a pretty safe bet he was getting ready to dump me. Who knows? Maybe he was just going to keep up with the two lives bit."

"Ohmygod," Paul says and rubs his hand down his face, like this information is too much for even him to process. I know the feeling. "You would think that his mom would have latched onto you, being that Carson is the only part of her son left in the world."

"Oh noooooo." I shake my head exaggeratedly. "Quite the contrary. When I went to quietly apply for survivor's benefits to help with Carson's care, she sent an attorney to block it in court. It should have been a no-brainer. He is the only survivor of Spence. But instead, there they were, claiming there was no proof Carson was his and therefore the state shouldn't have to pay any support."

Paul's jaw drops. "What the hell? Couldn't they do a DNA test?"

"Sure. Except her attorney took advantage of a notoriously slow court system and kept finding ways to make it hard to access any DNA."

"I…" Paul stumbles over his words, likely trying to process all this information. "I don't know what to say."

I shrug. I wouldn't say I'm necessarily over it. You don't just get over something like that. You do, however, move on.

"Survivors benefits mean a paper trail. Gotta make sure the other family never finds out about the bastard child or else it could cause problems with the companies and their shareholders, right?"

"But… what about Carson?"

I just nod. He's likely feeling a small portion of the indignation I felt the first two and a half years of Carson's life.

"The court saw through all that right?" Paul practically pleads. "Told her to fuck off or whatever and gave you the benefits?"

I shake my head slowly and Paul mutters a "shit," likely as disappointed as I was.

"Her attorney just kept dragging it out. Two years later, I guess she'd had enough and came to me with an *opportunity*. Fifteen grand if I would disappear and never speak of Spence again."

If it's possible, Paul's jaw falls even farther. "Please tell me you told her to fuck off."

I sigh and shift my feet. This is the part of the story where I'm never quite sure if I made the right decision or not. Too late to question myself now. "Nope. I took the money and I moved here."

He furrows his brow, obviously confused by my decision. "But… why?"

"It was a hard decision. Please don't misunderstand that. But in the end, it was about Carson, not me and my pride or her and her deceptions. When I did the math knowing Spence had never really worked before, the money she offered me was significantly more than I would have gotten over the entire eighteen years and in a lump sum. It was enough to finally move here where my support system is and still have a little bit of a cushion."

Paul shakes his head and I can't tell if he's disappointed in me or what. It doesn't really matter. It was my decision to make and until he's stuck in a situation where he's trying to feed his child and keep a roof over his head, it's not something he will ever be able to fully understand.

He finally looks at me, distress written all over his face, and in a few short seconds, he surprises the shit out of me by taking two steps forward and pulling me to his chest. His strong arms wrap around me and pull me even tighter to him, if that's possible. My heart beats rapidly at the contact.

"I'm so sorry that happened to you," he whispers into my hair and I can't help myself. My arms wrap around his waist against my better judgment. This is my boss. I know I shouldn't melt into him. But it feels good to have him hold me. Like I'm finally safe. Like I'm finally home.

I push my competing thoughts away and just revel in the most content feeling I've had in a while.

We stay like that for a few seconds until someone wolf

whistles across the room and yells, "When you're done with your canoodling, can ya bring me another fruity drink?"

I giggle and we slowly break apart.

"Sorry about that." Paul takes two quick steps back and shoves his hands in his pockets. "That was, um… I crossed a line. You have my apologies."

"Nothing to apologize for." I quickly turn away not wanting him to see that I liked it a little more than I should have. "If anything, I should be apologizing to Dwayne for not keeping him hydrated."

Paul chuckles, and the sound is even better than before, now that I know what it feels like to be pressed close to that chest. "Well, let him know I'll pay closer attention next time." Grabbing the ale from the fridge, he pops the top off and hands me the bottle. I slide under the counter and try to refocus on my job, but I already know it's a futile attempt. My thoughts are going to stay solidly in the moment when Paul's arms were wrapped around me and everything was right in my world.

Maybe it's a good thing we don't have many customers after all.

THIRTEEN
Paul

I have always wondered about Kiersten's back story. I've noticed her exhaustion. Even when she smiles and hustles around the room, it sits behind her eyes.

When I met Carson the other day, I thought I had it figured out. Moms in general are exhausted. My own mother claims she never slept until her kids finally moved out of the house. She's said more than once that she misses having a bustling household, but her body feels better than it ever did when everyone lived at home.

I also know they tend to do double duty from watching my mother after my douchebag of a father finally left us because of what disappointments we were to him. I assumed that's what I was seeing in Kiersten. That the weight of the world she carries on her shoulders is the result of having to deal with a deadbeat dad. It turns out, there is so much more to the situation than I knew. It breaks my heart for her and makes me livid at the same time. Guys are such dicks. This is partially why I haven't dated in a while. I never want to cause anyone to have that kind of sadness.

Especially not if my interest level stayed mostly in the primal territory.

The other part is because I've been too busy working my ass off to succeed. Failure is not an option. My mom and I may not be super close, but she sacrificed too much for me not to make something of myself.

Still, even after our heart-to-heart when Kiersten bared some of her deepest shame to me, she got right back to work keeping our regulars happy. Maybe a little too happy if you ask me. That's the primal side of me talking again.

Kiersten laughs as she spins on the dance floor, doing her best to two-step with Dwayne who is more than delighted to be her dance partner. I don't blame him. If it wouldn't be crossing yet another line, I'd be cutting in. But I've already pressed the boundaries once tonight.

The door opens and I instinctively call, "Welcome to Frui Vita." And then I look up, surprised to see a familiar face as Heath sidles up to the bar and sits down.

"Hey man," I greet excitedly as we shake hands. "What brings you to our neighborhood?"

"I'm friends with the owner," he says with a relaxed smile. "I thought I'd swing by and grab that free drink offered me the other day."

"You got it. What can I get ya?"

"Got any recommendations?"

"It's gonna depend on if you want beer or liquor. Pick your poison and I'll take it from there."

He blows out a breath as he considers. "I think I'll go for the hard stuff tonight."

"Long day?"

He shakes his head and drops his shoulders. "I swear Carson is more exhausting than training camp."

I can't help laughing at his assessment. It was pretty

hilarious watching a two-foot-tall kid drag this giant man around the other day.

Patting the bar with an "I got you covered", I push off to grab Absinth, whiskey, and some bitters. I make quick work of mixing and pouring, then place it down in front of our newest customer.

"Mmmmmm," he finally says with a lick of his lips. "That's pretty smooth. What is it?"

"It's called a Sazerac. Our regulars don't stray much from beer so I don't get to make it much. But I thought I remembered you drinking whiskey at the barbecue. I figured this might be something just different enough for a night out with friends. Or are you out by yourself tonight?"

He sips again before answering. "Nah. They're on the way. You met a couple of the guys the other night. Alex and Frankie are definitely coming. They may have invited some more but I'm not sure. Should be here soon."

"Nice," I say with a genuine smile. Three new customers aren't much, but it's a start. "I appreciate you guys coming here."

Heath swivels in his chair and chuckles under his breath when he sees Kiersten. "Why am I not surprised that one is cuttin' a rug instead of serving drinks."

"Hey, whatever keeps the customers content. And giving old Dwayne over there…" I tilt my chin in Dwayne's direction, "…a little attention keeps him pretty damn happy."

"I'm sure." Heath laughs again. "He could do worse than a hot brunette who dances with him on her breaks."

Yeah, he could. I can't help but stop and watch as she moves on the dancefloor. She's graceful and lithe. Her body instinctually finding the beat of some Top 40 hit as her arms flow elegantly above her head. I don't even hear whatever song is playing, singularly focused on watching her.

Until a throat clears next to me.

"You could do worse than her, too."

"Yeah." It takes me a second to register his words. "Wait, what?" I quickly turn to decide if he just eluded to what I think he eluded to. Based on the eyebrow that's raised and the way he won't make eye contact with me, I think he did. I huff a small laugh. "She's my employee, man. I couldn't go there even if I wanted to."

He turns and places the drink on the counter, leaning on his elbows and staring me straight in the eye. "But you want to."

I open my mouth and close it again. You can't bullshit a guy like Heath Germaine and I've been battling my own feelings for so long, I don't really want to.

Instead, I sigh and look back at the woman I've been pining over as she smiles at her dance partner. "Who wouldn't. She's pretty damn special."

"What's stopping you?"

"I told you. She's my employee. And she's really young."

"Age is just a number and Kiersten's got an old soul. And don't even get me started on office romances. They happen all the time. Haven't you ever seen the Hallmark channel? Office romance is everywhere. This is just an unconventional office."

I flip the towel off my shoulder and begin wiping down the bar. It's already spotless, but I need to do something with my hands. "I just took over this place a few months ago. I don't want to get a reputation for dating my staff. And I really don't want any drama if things go south. The last thing I need is to drive customers away like that."

Heath downs the rest of his drink and gestures for another. "Kiersten has already had her fair share of drama. The last person who you have to worry about that with is her."

"That's exactly my point." I grab the liquor I need again and begin mixing. "After everything that went on before, she doesn't need some old guy like me creating more problems for her."

Heath cocks his head to the side. "She told you."

I shrug. "Didn't know it was a secret."

"It's not. But she prefers to keep it under wraps since people tend to assume things about her the second they find out about the fiancée."

Guilt hits me in the gut, knowing I was one of those people. It was only for a second, but it still wasn't my finest moment.

"She must trust you if she told you the whole story. And she doesn't trust a lot of people. Take that for what it's worth."

I nod in understanding and finish making his Sazerac. He sips and sighs with contentment remarking again on how smooth it is. I do a quick check to make sure I have enough liquor to make several more of those. If more whiskey drinkers are coming, I need to be ready.

A few minutes and some small talk later, the woman in question comes bounding up to the bar.

Shoving Heath playfully, she asks, "What are you doing here? Aren't you babysitting tonight?"

He just shakes his head. "Your kid is killing me."

She huffs. "Oh please. You're the one who spoils him rotten. You created the little monster."

"I did. And I have no regrets. But when Annika showed up at my house, I took the opportunity to leave for a while.

This is the longest I've sat down all day."

Kiersten squeezes his shoulder in a gesture of their close friendship. I have an odd feeling of gratitude toward him for taking care of this amazing woman and her child.

"Poor baby," she chides. "The big bad football player being run ragged by a toddler."

"Thank you for your sympathy," he responds dryly.

"I hope my child hasn't driven you to drink alone. That's not good for you."

"Actually, I'm waiting for a couple of friends."

"Speaking of," I interject. "I need to grab another couple of bottles out of the back. Can you keep an eye on things up here for a second, Kiersten?"

"Sure." She slides under the counter, still bantering back and forth with her friend.

I take the few free minutes I have to use the facilities and grab a couple of bottles of the higher end liquor. This may be the only time we get some people with money in this place and I don't want to let them down by serving the cheap stuff.

By the time I get back, two men I recognize from our brief introductions at the barbecue have arrived. Kiersten already has them served and they seem to be enjoying themselves.

"Welcome gentlemen," I say as I put the bottles away.

"Thanks for having us," one of them, I think Alex, says raising his glass in salute.

"Heath mentioned this was a low-key place to hang out," the other guy, Frankie I presume, mentions. "It's uh… interesting."

I laugh, wondering what he sees as a first-time customer. "Yeah, it's definitely got a bit of multiple personalities to it right now."

"I was telling them you have some plans drawn up to spruce the place up a bit. You should show them." Kiersten nudges me with her shoulder, then grabs another ale and takes off to deliver it. I assume Dwayne is thirsty yet again.

I'm not really sure they care, but all three of them claim to be interested. What the hell?

Pulling out the very rough blueprints I've drawn up, I place them in from of the guys. "You may not be able to read those. I can't afford to hire a professional, so I had to draw them up myself. I'm hoping to get it started in a couple weeks."

Heath looks closely at my drawings. "You're doing the work yourself?"

"We're not exactly rolling in customers right now," I admit sheepishly. It's not abnormal for a business to start out slow, but it's still a bit discouraging sometimes. "I have to get it done as cheaply as possible."

"What are you needing done?" Frankie asks as he looks around the room. I wonder if he's trying to envision changes.

"For starters, I need to get rid of that damn railing."

I point to the offending spindles and Heath laughs. "Yeah, it is a bit strange to have it in the middle of the room."

"Once it's gone, we want to pull down the extension on the stage, move the dance floor over, and give the whole place a fresh coat of paint. I've got some new furniture coming that should bring the whole room out of the 80s and make it a little more modern."

"You need some help?"

I look at Heath, taken aback. "Really?"

"Well, let's think about this. We head to training next week." Frankie and Alex nod. Are they offering to help, too? "If there's any way to do it this coming weekend, we don't have anything else to do. At least I don't. What about you guys?"

"Nah man." Alex finishes his drink and sets the glass on the counter. "I was just going to hang around the house and rest up. But it sounds more fun to do some demo. It always looks fun on TV anyway."

"I could break some things," Frankie adds. "Is that too soon for you?"

I'm stunned by their offers of help. I assumed I would be doing most of this alone. This is much better. "Yeah. I mean no. I can get all the supplies by Saturday if you guys are serious. That would be great. I can pay you in pizza and beer."

"Sold." Frankie rubs his abs. "Although I'm warning you, I can pack away a lot of pizza."

The group laughs and begins ribbing each other about Frankie eating too much junk during the off-season. I'm only half-listening, too busy figuring out how to make this transition happen in the next couple of days instead of weeks. It'll be rough to coordinate but the actual work will go much faster. That alone makes the date shift worth it.

"Hey, man. I think we're going to head to a table," Heath says as the other guys stand up and walk toward a larger space. "A couple more guys are on the way so we want to spread out."

"Sure. If y'all need anything, please let me know. If anyone starts to harass you for autographs or selfies or whatever, grab either me or Kiersten. I'll escort them out, no questions asked."

Heath furrows his brow. "You don't want this place all over social media? Could be some good marketing for you."

I shrug. "I'm not opposed to advertising and I want my business to do well and all, but not at the expense of my customers. I would rather you guys have a place to just chill without worrying about all that public nonsense."

"Thanks, man. And don't worry. We got you covered with the renovations." He points at me as he walks away to rejoin his group.

A take a deep breath and squelch my excitement. This is exactly the break I've been looking for. And I have Kiersten to thank for all of it.

FOURTEEN

Kiersten

The crunch under my feet is a reminder of how loved my son is. It's also a reminder of how much cleaning I have to do. My apartment is trashed with wrapping paper, bits of tape, and paper plates. This is going to take hours to clean up.

For Carson's third birthday party, we invited a few friends over for lunch and cake. Lauren offered to make good on Heath's promise to have it at their house, where we could spread out more, but as much as I love being there, sometimes I just want to entertain in my own space. It's definitely easier to put presents away without having to haul them home first.

As he's been doing for the last fifteen minutes or so, the birthday boy comes racing into the living room. "Gimme twase, mommy."

"Give me trash, please," I remind him sternly. Again. We've had this exact same conversation at least a dozen times already.

He holds his hand out to me, completely unaffected by

my tone or my correction. "Gimme twase, pweeze, mommy."

I hand him the largest piece of wrapping paper I can find hoping it entertains him for a while. His latest obsession is throwing away trash. I don't understand the excitement that comes with picking a piece of lint off the floor and tossing it in the bin, but I freely admit the apartment floor has never looked cleaner.

I smile when my sister Nicole rounds the corner from the bathroom and begins helping me breakdown boxes for the dumpster. I love having her here. I've missed her.

"I can't believe he got this much stuff for his birthday."

She's obviously never been around my friends.

"Yeah, they like to spoil him."

Clearly, she does, too. When I mentioned the small party for Carson, Nicole immediately decided to make the five-hour drive from her school so she didn't miss it, despite it being on a Friday evening and her having an afternoon class. He and I were both thrilled when she arrived this afternoon, just in time for the evening festivities.

It wasn't ideal to have a Friday night birthday party, but since I have to be at work early tomorrow morning for our first day of renovations, it fit my schedule the best. And it wasn't terribly difficult for everyone else to meet us after work hours at the small park across the street for some fun.

I assumed it would just be the few friends we have, but as always, Uncle Heath went above and beyond. When a giant bounce house and a guy with a pony showed up, all the neighborhood kids came out to play.

We ended up meeting a lot of new people and stayed outside a lot longer than I anticipated. We didn't even come inside for cake and ice cream until the bouncy house was packed up and driven away. I'm hoping it's the first of many impromptu block parties.

Nicole sighs. "I just love that you guys have created a family here. A healthy one with people who don't continually remind you of your mistakes."

I plop down on the couch, suddenly tired of being on my feet. You'd think I'd be physically used to it by now with my job. Apparently not. "Uh oh. What is mom ranting about now?"

Nicole bites her lip and I know whatever my mother has latched onto isn't good. "I'm dating someone."

I gasp, excited to hear all about it. "Oh, that's great. What's his name? What's his major? Is he wonderful?"

A smile crosses her face and I almost get teary thinking about my baby sister in love for the first time. "His name is Jeremy and he's a freshman like me."

Forgetting the boxes, I turn on the couch and bring my knees to my chest. "Tell me everything."

Nicole blushes prettily. She's always been the more attractive of the two of us in my eyes. Where I'm a skinny brunette, she's a curvy blonde. Where I can't draw a straight line with eyeliner to save my life, she looks glam every day. She fits the "Texas ideal" way more than I ever have. She's also the sweetest person I've ever known. It's one of the reasons I love her so much.

"There's not much to tell, really." I can tell by her tone she's lying, but this is her story to tell. How much she wants to share is fine. "He hasn't decided on a major yet, but he's got time. He likes to take me out to dinner and dancing. Says he likes showing me off. And he never leaves me alone when we go to parties." Her cheeks redden. She's obviously smitten. I'm happy for her.

"Sounds like he really likes you."

"I think so." She licks her bottom lip. "Actually, I know

so. We're kind of fighting right now. You probably heard my phone blowing up all night."

"I didn't notice. Too many kids were screaming. What are you arguing about?"

"Nothing much. I'm sure we'll work it out," she says quickly. "But anyway, mom knows about him and every time he comes up in our conversations, she reminds me that I better not have a baby out of wedlock like you did."

Sounds exactly like my mom—never focusing on the human being who is currently picking up tiny pieces of tape off the floor, just remembering the "unplanned" part.

"As infuriating as she is, we've already talked about this." I'm not at all offended by my mom's judgment. I'm used to it by now. "You know how to have safe sex."

The blush is back, my sweet sister being easily embarrassed. "Kiersten. Carson is in the room."

I look over at my child is who is paying us no attention at all. Apparently one of the pieces of tape is stuck to the carpet. He could be there for hours.

"Sex isn't a bad word, Nicole. It's part of life. Neither is the word *condoms*. Are you stocked up on those?"

She quietly clears her throat. "I'm actually on the pill. Mom made sure of it."

I purse my lips. "You're smarter than that. You know that's not the only thing condoms are used for. Or do I need to remind you?"

"No. No, I know. And yes, I have them if I need them."

"Good." I grab her hand and squeeze. "I love you too much for anything to happen to you, ya know?"

She squeezes back and I'm even more appreciative that's she's here, knowing she sacrificed her weekend with her boyfriend to be here with us, sleeping on the couch. Come to think of it, I should probably be the one sleeping on the couch since I'm the one who gets home late.

"I know. I promise I'm being safe."

I nod once, her answer good enough for me. Unlike my mom, I trust my sister to be an adult. Even if she were to get pregnant accidentally, she'd handle it flawlessly. And I'd be right by her side the whole time.

"NicNic!" Carson shouts holding a book over his head. By his reaction, it seems he accidentally found this new treasure under the wrapping paper. "NicNic, read to me."

"Carson…" I warn because he *knows* how to say please. He just thinks he doesn't have to say it. This is proving to be a hard habit to break.

"NicNic, pweese."

Nicole giggles. "Of course, sweet boy. Come sit next to me and I'll read you your book."

He climbs up on her lap and giggles as she snuggles him before settling in together.

"Let's see what book you have. Oh, it's called *Teddy Bear's Travels*." Nicole sounds excited to be reading a children's book. For most people, I would say it was for show, but knowing my sister, she really is excited. I know she hasn't declared her major yet, but my money is on early childhood education.

"Teddy Bear lived in a big house with his very best friend, JT," she reads, Carson relaxed against her as he looks at the pictures.

I smile at their easy interaction. Nicole spent more than two years as my regular babysitter. Living here means things are a lot easier with having more support, but if I could, I'd help my sister transfer to the local college in a second if it meant her being here with us.

"He on da bus!" Carson yells and points at the picture.

"He is on the bus." Nicole smiles encouragingly at

him, pointing out various parts of the picture before she continues reading. "So Daddy, the little girl, and Teddy Bear all walked down the street to the corner, where they waited for the bus."

Satisfied I have a few minutes before Carson is off like a tornado again, I resume clean up. I'm glad we used paper plates because they're easy to throw away. But I'm not looking forward to how many trips to the dumpster I'm going to have to make.

"Wheya daddy?"

My movements stutter at Carson's question. Why is he asking about the daddy? My heart begins beating a little faster, feeling like we're on the precipice of something huge.

Nicole looks up at me, eyes wide. It only lasts half a second before she tries to play it off. "He's right there, see? He's sitting next to Teddy Bear on the bus."

She starts reading again but Carson seems to have other things on his mind.

"No. Wheya my daddy?"

My heart plummets. I knew he would ask this question eventually I just wasn't expecting it so soon. What's the right answer? I don't want to lie to him, but the truth is really heavy for a three-year-old to process. Quickly running through the options, I decide the best answer is just the truth—simplified a bit.

Sitting next to him, I rub his little back. "Carson, your daddy is in heaven, baby. With the angels."

Carson's big brown eyes stare at me as he thinks through the information I just gave him. Then he turns back to the book. "No. Unca Heat my daddy."

I laugh. I laugh at his innocence. I laugh at his easy reasoning. I laugh because Heath would get a kick out of it. But once I'm done laughing, I know I have to make sure he understands the truth.

Sitting down on the couch, I rub his little leg. "Baby, Uncle Heath isn't your daddy. He's your *uncle*. And he loves you so much and loves playing with you and swimming and mowing the lawn."

"I go swimming, mama."

I should have expected him to latch onto his favorite activity. Maybe distraction is the best thing right now until I figure out more answers. Unfortunately, I have more bad news. "That sounds fun, but Uncle Heath isn't at home, baby, remember? He's playing football."

In true toddler fashion, Carson throws himself backward, his arms over his head, his bottom half hanging off the couch. And then he begins screaming. "No! I swimming! I go swimming!"

"Carson," I say calmly, having learned that when I raise my voice, he only gets louder. "How about we Skype Uncle Heath and he can show you where he is."

I have no idea what Heath's schedule is like right now but I have no doubt he'll answer if he can. Skyping with Carson was a regular thing before we moved and they had the most fun making faces at each other through the camera. I'm sure nothing has changed.

"No, I swimming!"

"I know," Nicole announces out of nowhere. "Let's go swimming." Carson immediately stops screaming, probably trying to decide if she's yanking his chain.

He narrows his eyes in question. "I swimming?"

She smiles and claps her hands together. "Yes. Let's go swimming… in the bathtub."

Carson slithers the rest of the way off the couch and begins jumping up and down. "I go swimming, NicNic."

I drop my chin to my chest. That was too easy. I really should have thought of that one before.

Nicole laughs and pats my shoulder. "Don't worry about it. I'll take him."

I nod gratefully and watch as they bound down the small hallway. It was a pretty ingenious idea. If only she could figure out the answers to those harder questions, I'd be set.

FIFTEEN
Paul

The day I've been planning is finally here—Demo Day. I am equal parts excited and dreading all this work. I've got sledgehammers, paint, and a rental dumpster outside to clear out all the trash. I also have a lot of various tools we may need, depending on what we find. That part is where the dread comes in. While the inspection before the sale went off without a hitch, you never know what will pop up when things start being dismantled. I've already spent a pretty penny on supplies. Fingers crossed we don't run into any major problems that require professionals.

"I'm here!"

Kiersten races through the door, out of breath from what I presume was a run across the parking lot. "I'm sorry. I didn't hear my alarm go off. It wasn't until Carson jumped on me that I woke up."

"Did you leave him at home or something?"

She laughs lighting. "My sister is in town so she's keeping him for the day. Which makes me feel even worse about being late. I have no excuses except my body clock is all mixed up right now. I guess switching over to working nights was easier than I thought it would be."

"Don't worry about the time," I say trying not to notice the white tank top she's wearing that pulls a little too tight across her chest. It's distracting me already and she just got here. "Coffee is fresh. We're just waiting for the muscle to arrive so we can get started."

She takes a deep breath and puts her hand on my arm. Like every time she touches me, it feels like a lightning current runs through my body at the contact. "Thank you. I didn't have time to grab any on my way out. I'll be right back."

She heads to the office to drop off her things, just in time for Heath to approach. I didn't even know he was here yet. Shows how much I notice things around me when Kiersten is around.

Standing next to me, facing the same direction I am, he crosses his arms, and lets out a "Hmmph."

I don't bother looking at him. I know what that sound means and I can see his smirk out of the corner of my eye. "You can keep your commentary to yourself."

"I didn't say anything about your crush on my friend."

"You didn't have to. Besides, we have bigger issues today. Like dismantling that stage."

Now he looks at me. Only this time it's with dismay. "What? I'm here for the demo, man. Where's my sledgehammer?"

"We'll get to it, I promise. But I kind of need to see what we're dealing with under there first. If we find any extra issues, I need to know quickly."

"Yeah, I hear ya." Blowing out a breath, he moves his head side to side, cracking his neck. "Okay. Let's do it." Grabbing a drill, Heath takes off to start figuring out how to take the stage apart.

In less than half an hour, close to a dozen people are here and everyone has had a shot or two of caffeine. Things are rolling and there's no going back now.

Kiersten and Annika are moving out the old furniture and decide to post it for sale on some social media site. I appreciate their ingenuity since I was just going to throw it in the dumpster. Bringing in some cash for it is a better idea. It won't be much, but it'll at least pay to feed all these people.

Lauren, who apparently needs to work out some rage over a disagreement with her boss or something, convinced Jaxon to show her how to use a sledgehammer and is now having way too much fun tearing down the weird railing. Every once in a while, I have to duck when debris comes flying. Like I said—*way* too much fun.

And the three football players are taking advantage of their upper body strength to pull panels apart and set them aside. From their grunts, I assume it's heavier than it looks.

Satisfied we're well on our way to getting things done, I grab a can of black paint and begin prepping to update the bar area a bit.

"Hey, boss. I'm here. Whatcha need me to do?" an unexpected straggler says.

Surprised, I greet Tammy with a hug. "What are you doing here? I told you not to worry about helping out today. It's your day off with the hubs."

"He picked up an extra shift so I didn't have nothing better to do. Besides," she smacks me on the chest lightly with a scowl. "I may be old enough to be your mama, but I'm not dead. I know there's something I can do around here to help."

I snicker. This is why Tammy has been an employee

here for years. She's a hard worker no matter what the task. Still, we've got professional athletes that can do the heavy lifting. No reason for her to throw her back out. Besides, I can't afford a ding on workman's comp.

"If you can help me prep to paint the front of the bar, that would be great. Then it's probably cleaning the floors where the stage used to be."

As if she noticed the newly cleared area, her eyes widen. "Oh wow. That's gonna be a huge change."

"We're going for a modern update. Fingers crossed this will do the trick."

• • •

Hours later, maybe two, maybe ten, who knows at this point, I sign off on the delivery of the new furniture, thanking the guys who hauled it all in.

I can't believe how different this place looks already. It's better than I imagined it would be. With most of the stage and the odd railing gone, we were able to move the dance floor over by several feet. Even with the new furniture that includes a few booths, it already feels more open.

The black paint on the face of the bar makes the wood of the countertop pop. And the black trim gives the back bar some sprucing up and brings out it of the 70s.

We also added some dark tint to the windows. We still get a lot of light during the day, but at night, it'll hopefully give the inside a little more privacy. The only things left to do now is a quick coat of paint on the main walls, a good floor cleaning, and changing out the light fixtures. But first, nourishment. Jaxon and Annika walk in, right on time.

"Who's hungry?" he yells and drops a dozen pizza boxes on the counter.

What can only be described as a roar breaks out among

the guys and they barrel toward the food. Kiersten and I slip behind the counter and begin making drinks behind the bar as everyone places their orders.

"Thanks for the food," Annika says kindly before taking a huge bite and groaning in delight.

A few more people grumble their thanks around their food.

"It's the least I could do. There is no way I would have accomplished this much on my own in a day."

"It really looks great in here," Kiersten remarks as she slides Lauren an Apple Pie ale. "Is this the vibe you were looking for?"

"Pretty close, yeah."

At first, I was nervous about doing black paint in a room with so much wood. But after Kiersten showed me some pictures she found on the internet, I decided to go for it. It makes the room a little more updated without losing some of the country feel.

"Yo, this place is looking hot." I hand Alex a bottle of Dos Equis. "As soon as we get back from training camp, we need to bring the team here for some downtime." Frankie and Heath nod in agreement, still concentrating on their food. Pretty sure they've already inhaled three large pizzas.

"Just so you know, I'm staking my claim on that booth right there. You might as well put my name on it, Paul." Frankie points at the black high back booth facing what's left of the stage. I sprung for a slightly more expensive design, specifically so it would be comfortable. I want the guests here to want to hang around.

Once the pizza is gone, we hang out for a long while, relaxing our sore muscles and enjoying the company and cold beverages. Through all the chatter, I hear someone decide we need to test out the dance floor in its new location. Before I know it, music is piping through the speakers. Judging by the song choice, my guess is Tammy is the one itching to dance. She's the only one I know who would pick a song this old.

"Come on young pup." She holds a hand out to Alex. "Let this old dog show you some new tricks." He quickly humors her and in a matter of seconds, they're laughing like old friends as she teaches him to two-step. He's terrible at it.

"For someone who practically dances across that field, he sure is a shitty dancer," Lauren says with a laugh.

"I doubt you'd be much better at country dancing, short stuff." Heath grabs her by the hand. "Let's go find out." With their height difference, it doesn't go well and pretty soon they give up the traditional way of dancing, Heath picking up Lauren who wraps her legs around his waist. It looks funny, but at least he's not bent in half anymore.

Jaxon and Annika aren't far behind them and soon several couples are laughing and swaying, partially dancing and partially stumbling around from too much beer. Except for Frankie. He's already made himself comfortable in the booth as promised, bobbing his head to the music.

Turning to Kiersten, I lift one eyebrow. "Feel like dancing?"

A smile slowly creeps up her face. "I thought you'd never ask."

I take her hand in mine, trying hard to ignore the tingle on my skin. After so many weeks of wanting to touch her, of having to hold myself back, my awareness of this little bit of contact is heightened.

Unwilling to make a fool of myself by trying to two-step, I just pull her close, our clasped hands pressed between us, and we begin to sway.

"Are you glad to have this finally done?" she asks quietly as we ignore the others around us.

"There's still a few more things to do, but I didn't expect us to get this far in one day. If I'd known, I wouldn't have told Dwayne not to come back until Monday."

Kiersten giggles. "He's not going to recognize the place. But I kind of hope he takes to the pool table. The more he drinks, the more nervous I get about stray darts."

"Yeah, that may not have been my best idea."

She laughs again and lays her head on my chest. I try to resist, but I can't help it and rest my own head on hers. She smells like whatever vanilla hair product she uses and lightly of some perfumed scent, but I can't put a finger on what it is.

Regardless, the feel of her body being so close practically makes me hard. That's a problem. This attraction is problematic in general. She's my employee. She's a single mom. She's eleven years younger than me even if she does act older and wiser than her years.

But no matter how much my head tries to justify staying far away from her, neither my body nor my heart will listen.

Pulling back, Kiersten looks up at me, her bright brown eyes practically boring into my heart.

"Thank you, Paul."

"For what?"

"Everything really. But mostly for trusting me with this job. I know I was a long shot since I didn't have any experience, but it turns out this is my favorite place to be."

"Unless it's with Carson, of course." I smile as I say it. I love watching her face light up at the thought of her son.

"Of course. But being here is a really great thing, too. I

miss teaching dance. That's my passion. But I love the customers and I like working with Tammy. And I like working with you."

She bites her lip and I know she thinks she's said too much. She probably has. This chemistry we feel can never be anymore more than that—a feeling. Acting on it would create so many problems for both of us. She needs a man who can provide for her and Carson without her having to pull the night shift at a bar. Carson needs a man who can step into the role of father and have the time and schedule to coach little league and take him camping. Neither of those are things I can provide them.

And yet, I can't stop staring at that bottom lip she's biting. Or her tongue when it peeks out to smooth over the indented skin.

Mesmerized by this amazing woman, I feel myself leaning in closer. I should stop myself. I should. But I don't. I keep inching toward her, our faces mere centimeters apart. My nose brushes hers, our breath intermingling. Just a little closer…

"AHEM," a loud voice calls and I immediately break out of my daze, pulling away from the one person I want to keep holding.

"Heath!" Lauren chides as they dance up to us. "That was rude."

Heath leans in when they get close enough and he stares straight at me with a conspiratorial smirk. "Nothing to worry about, huh?" and then they dance away, Lauren still berating him. He doesn't seem to care that she's not happy with him, nor does he seem to care that calling me out has embarrassed Kiersten and I both.

Shoving my hands in my pockets, I look at the floor, not sure what to say besides, "I'm sorry. I almost crossed a line."

When I finally glance up, I can see the hurt in Kiersten's eyes. Even with a smile affixed to her face, I know I've upset her.

"It's my fault," she says. "I got a little carried away with my gratitude, I guess."

We both know that's a lie, but if it helps smooth over this awkward moment, I won't call her out.

"Of course." I nod my head and my lips try to quirk up. They fail miserably. "We both just…" A sigh comes from deep within me because there's nothing left to say. "Yeah."

We stare at each other awkwardly, not quite sure of the best way to proceed. Finally, Frankie breaks the discomfort for us.

Reaching out his hand, he bows low and with a lot of exaggeration. "May I have this dance, milady?"

Kiersten's normal smile is back, the one that makes the customers light up and has me practically melting into a damn puddle. "I thought you'd never ask," she says dramatically with her hand over her heart, batting her eyelashes.

As I quickly leave the dance floor, so I don't get run over by the not-so-great dancers, I accidentally catch Tammy's eye. She winks at me.

That is exactly why I've tried to stay away from Kiersten. I only have one other employee at this point and the last thing we need is her either trying to play matchmaker or sticking her nose in the middle of a non-existent relationship.

Well shit.

SIXTEEN

Kiersten

"**P**aw Patwo! Paw Patwo! Wheneva yaw in twou-ba!" Carson sings from in front of the televi-sion. Actually, singing isn't the right word. Screaming is more like it. The walls in this place are thin so I have no idea how Nicole is sleeping through it. Carson must have run her ragged yesterday, which is saying a lot since I was the one doing the heavy lifting. Yet I was still the first one up this morning.

Then again, it wasn't like my thoughts would shut off overnight. I was too busy thinking about Paul and the sto-len touches while we were painting. The laughter as we worked. The easy banter we fall into every time we're to-gether.

And that almost kiss that had me wishing we could be more. But we can't be. Paul made it very clear that as the boss, he won't cross that line. And I have boundaries of my own—if someone doesn't want to put forth the effort to be with me and only me, it's not a relationship I'll pursue.

Instead, I'll just pine over him as I make breakfast, I

suppose. The part-singing-part-yelling has stopped so I glance up from the skillet where I'm making my son's favorite chocolate chip pancakes. He's now standing stock-still in front of the boob tube, mouth wide open, as he watches his favorite rescue workers learn how to share or something equally as preschool.

I laugh at how cute he is. If someone had told me five years ago that the love of my life would come in a pint-sized package that sleeps with this foot in my face and loves picking up garbage, well, I wouldn't have believed them. But there he is in all his footie pajama glory.

Still, it would be nice to be loved by a grown man, too, not just a little one.

And just like that my thoughts go right back to Paul, no matter how hard I try to push him out of my mind. But he's nice. And stable. And honorable. He's also really easy on the eyes. Even better, I hear how he talks to his customers and he treats his employees with such genuine respect and care. Even when it's his "off day," which means catching up on paperwork in the back, he doesn't want to hang out in his office. He wants to be behind the bar, serving people. Making them happy. I recognize how rare those qualities are and they make him all the more attractive to me. No matter how hard I pretend they don't.

Flipping the pancake over one more time to make sure it's fully cooked, I see Nicole come out of the bedroom, rubbing her eyes.

"Good morning." Her voice is groggy with sleep and I point to the old school coffee maker which has a fresh pot already made.

We're silent with the exception of the sounds of cartoons until she has a few sips of her first cup of joe. Nicole has never been a morning person. Neither have I, but my body clock is irrelevant these days.

She sits at the small table in silence until she's finally awake enough to hold a conversation. "Why are you only making one pancake at a time?"

Flipping it onto the growing stack, I pour batter into the skillet again before grabbing Carson's plate and cutting up his breakfast into bite sized chunks.

"Because I don't have a griddle. The skillet works fine, it just takes longer."

She grunts her response, taking another sip. "Why are you up early?"

"Unlike us, Carson is a morning person. He got me up bright and early."

Another grunt. "I don't believe you."

I look up at her, confused.

"I've known you my whole life, Kiersten. I can tell when something kept you up most of the night. And I suspect it has nothing to do with my nephew."

I gape at her and how much more astute she is than I gave her credit for.

"That's what I thought." She leans back on her chair, keeping a tight grip on her mug.

"For someone who is just waking up, you are awfully chatty this morning."

"No deflecting. What gives, Kiersten?"

I sigh and pour some syrup on the pancakes, walking the plate to the table before heading back to the stove. "I … sort of had a moment with my boss yesterday. I just can't get it off my mind."

"Explain what you mean by *a moment*."

I flip the pancake and bite my lip. It's one thing to be thinking about what happened. It's another to tell someone about it. As if verbalizing the moment makes it more real.

"Kiersten…"

I flip the stove off, dumping the final pancake onto the stack. "We almost kissed."

Her eyes go wide and she starts to choke on her coffee. Maybe I should have waited until she was done swallowing before blurting that part out.

Nicole pats her chest and coughs for a few more seconds before squeaking out, "Almost?"

I begin dishing out food, mostly to keep my hands busy while I tell her everything that has happened up until this point—the easy conversation at the barbecue, the smiles when no one is looking, the kiss that almost was until Heath interrupted. Nicole sits in rapt attention as I finally get all the details off my chest for the first time.

"Kiersten," she finally says when I'm done. "You're in love with him."

"What? I am not." Turning to the living room I yell for my son. "Carson, baby, breakfast. We have pancakes."

He comes shrieking into the room, chattering about some puppy that got stuck in a tree as he climbs onto his chair. I'm grateful for the reprieve but it only lasts a few seconds before he shoves so much food in his mouth he can't talk anymore.

I join them at the table, giving Nicole a plate and tucking into my own food. Looking up, I see her just staring at me.

"What?"

One of her eyebrows raises. That's it. That's all I get from her. Unfortunately, as her sister, I know what that means, and in a nutshell, she's not letting this go.

I finally roll my eyes, giving up. "It's not love. We don't know each other well enough." My voice quiets as I admit the one thing I haven't even said to myself yet.

"But… it… could be. Eventually."

"I knew it!" she shouts and Carson looks up from his plate.

"Know what, NicNic?" he asks around a mouthful of food, blowing crumbs as he talks.

"Knew your mommy is a big fat liar."

He looks over at me, his eyes glancing over my whole body. "Mommy not fat."

I ruffle his hair, laughing at how literal he takes things.

"You're right," Nicole admits. "But she is a liar." Turning back to me, she crosses her arms over her chest. "So, what's the problem?"

"You know the problem. I already told you."

"What? That he's your boss? That he's older than you? So what? From everything you've said he sounds amazing."

"He is." I can admit that much. "But he also has made it very clear that there is a no fraternization policy at work and that means even for him."

Nicole takes a bite of her pancakes while making a noise that can only be interpreted as disagreement. "That is a load of crap. He made the rules. He can break the rules. He just needs you to give him a reason."

"No way. I'm not in the game of trying to convince a man why I'm good enough for him. I either am or I'm not. But I don't have time to play games. I will never do that again."

She lifts her sleeve to scratch her shoulder and that's when I see it. Bruises. Bright yellow and purple bruises on her bicep. My heart drops and my whole body runs cold. That can't be what I think it is. Oh please, don't let that be what I think it is.

"Nic," I say slowly, my eyes glued to her arm. "What

happened?"

Looking down at where her shirt is raised, Nicole's face reddens and she pulls her sleeve down quickly, stumbling over her words. "Oh um. I fell."

"You fell." I've heard this excuse before and only on television or in movies. It's practically a giveaway for a domestic violence situation. The look on her face, her terrified expression, her refusal to make eye contact are even bigger clues that she's lying to me. "Nicole, it looks like you have bruises in the shape of finger marks on your arm."

"What? No. It was at the gym. I fell over a weight on the floor and rammed my arms into this weird machine. It had this odd sort of shape. I hit it just right. I'm fine. It's fine. Don't worry about me."

She keeps yanking on her sleeve, making sure it's in place. And suddenly weird comments she's made for the last couple of months start flooding back to me. Like how Jeremy refuses to leave her side at parties. How he likes "showing her off" in public. How she made last second plans to visit using Carson's birthday as an excuse even though it's such a long drive. How her phone has been blowing up all weekend and she refuses to answer unless she's in private.

I can't believe this. My baby sister is dating a guy who abuses her. I have no doubt. I just don't know what to do about it.

"Nicole," I say slowly trying not to scare her off. I'm not sure what else to do. "It's not fine. Those are finger marks from someone putting their hands on you. Was it Jeremy? Are you afraid of him? If you need to stay here for a while—"

"I'm not lying," she interrupts a little too quickly. "You don't know. You've never even met him. Don't accuse him of something like this. I swear I was at the gym and I *fell*."

I nod slowly, unconvinced but needing some time to regroup. She's safe for the moment. "Okay. But you know if you need something, or if you're afraid or can't get out, I'll do anything to help you."

She slams her fork onto the table, which is completely uncharacteristic for her normally even keel demeanor. "I don't need your help." Pushing away from the table, she quietly adds, "I have to hit the road soon. I'm going to take a shower."

I watch her storm off, slamming the bathroom door closed behind her.

Having lost my appetite, I drop my fork on my plate. Of all the issues I ever expected my sister to have, being in an abusive relationship is never one that crossed my mind. I have no idea what I'm supposed to do now.

SEVENTEEN
Paul

It's technically my day off and I should be sleeping away the weekend of manual labor, but I want to be here for the grand re-opening today.

There's not actually a celebration beyond my own excitement. Banners and streamers were not only out of my budget but didn't seem necessary. Mostly I want to be here to see the reaction on people's faces when they see the updates. Plus, we still have a little bit of organization to do on the shelves and I'd like to get that all done.

Having been employed here longer than the rest of us, Tammy knows pretty much all the history of this place. And she says she doesn't remember the last time there was a fresh coat of paint on the walls, let alone actual renovations, so the changes really seem to excite her. Personally, I think she just had a good time doting on all the football players this weekend and is still reveling in the memories of that day. Whatever keeps her happy while she's here.

On the other hand, something's wrong with Kiersten. She's been acting strange since she walked in the door, sort of downtrodden and distracted. It's a complete one-eighty from the other day. I want to ask her about it because I'm honestly worried about her, but we've been busy getting ready to open up I haven't had time. Plus, I'm not really sure it's my place. I shut her down pretty quick when we almost kissed. Drawing her back in seems like giving mixed signals.

As soon as the door is unlocked, it swings open and our numero uno patron comes walking in, right on cue. Before the door even closes behind him, he stops, mouth wide open in shock.

"Whoa," Dwayne breathes, as he looks around the room taking in all the changes.

"You like?" I call out, hoping he gives me the answer I want after all that time and money.

"I feel like I walked into a fancy place."

"You're about to have your mind blown then." Tammy points to the back corner next to the stage. "Check out the new pool table."

His eyes widen. "I love pool. Can I get one of those fancy ales, too?" he adds as he takes off across the room to check out the new set up.

"Coming right up," Kiersten replies before grabbing his drink from the small fridge. "Thank god for small miracles. I was sure he'd never leave that dartboard."

I blow out a breath, releasing some of the nervous tension I've been carrying around now that I know things are being well received. If Dwayne can be swayed, there's hope.

Over the next couple of hours, a few customers trickle in; some new, some familiar faces. The increased traffic probably has less to do with the number of people and more to do with them staying longer. That's exactly what I was hoping for when I splurged on comfortable furniture. So far, everything is going well for our first night post-reno.

The only downside is Kiersten. She can't seem to shake whatever mood she's in. Sure, she's smiled at all the right times and laughed at silly things, but I can see something else is going on. Several times, I've caught her wiping her eyes when she thinks no one is looking. Even now, as she rinses out the blender, it looks like she's about to cry.

I place Tammy's order on her tray and lean in to talk to her quietly. "Is everyone good for a few minutes? I need to talk to Kiersten privately."

"Yeah you do," she replies, keeping her voice low. That's unusual for my very boisterous lead waitress. If she's trying to be discreet, I know it's not just me noticing the change in attitude. Tammy glances around the room quickly to make sure none of her patrons will need a refill any time soon. "We'll be good for a bit. If it gets busy, I'll come get you. But you need to find out what's going on with that girl first."

I nod my thanks as she grabs her tray and hustles away. Taking a deep breath, I prepare myself to be shut down. If Kiersten doesn't want to talk, there's nothing I can do to force the issue. Still, I need to try. Even if it's just so she knows I'm here for her.

Walking up behind Kiersten, I lean in. "Hey," I say quietly. "Come with me for a second." She looks surprised when I grab her by the hand but doesn't pull away as I lead her into the office, closing the door behind us.

Turning to face her, I try not to get too much in her space, but I'm worried. "What's wrong."

She smiles, like I knew she would. It's fake and I still see the shimmer of pending tears. There aren't many, but they're there. "Nothing, I'm okay."

"I don't believe you, Kiersten. Something has you distracted and sad. I just want to help."

Sniffing once, she crosses her arms over her chest in a very obvious defensive stance. "Maybe I'm on my period."

The remark gets an incredulous look from me. "You've worked here for three months. By that logic, I should have seen this mood at least twice before, but I haven't."

She crinkles her nose. "That's kind of gross, Paul. That you would notice that kind of thing?"

Deflection is not her strong suit. I shrug my shoulders because, "I'm not trying to make it weird. I just want to know what's really happening."

Sighing deeply, she moves to the couch and sinks down onto it, putting her face in her hands. Now I'm really concerned.

"Is it Carson?" I ask, sitting next to her. Alarm bells are going off in my head. Please don't let it be her kid. "Is he okay?"

"He's fine," she says quickly, and I find myself breathing an unexpected sigh of relief. "As perfect as a three-year-old can be." She takes a shaky breath, still holding back tears. "It's my sister. I think… I'm almost positive, she's in an abusive relationship."

I suck in a breath, her mood making perfect sense now. "Oh, no."

"Oh, yeah."

Before I can stop myself, I wipe a stray tear off her cheek. She quickly sits upright and I immediately pull back, knowing I've made things awkward. Quickly, I grab a tissue box off my desk and hand it to her. "Are you sure? Did she say something about it?"

"I accidentally saw her arm when she lifted up her

sleeve. She has bruises, finger-shaped bruises on her bicep. She claims she fell into a piece of equipment at the gym but I know she's lying. Hell, that's not even a creative lie." Kiersten sniffles again and wipes more tears away. No wonder she's been "off" today. If I remember correctly, her sister only left yesterday to go back to school. I can't imagine how out of control this makes her feel.

"Have you talked to her since she left?"

Kiersten shakes her head. "She texted me just to say she made it back okay, but she didn't answer when I called."

"Wow." I shift my body, my hands resting on my knees. Now that I know there's no immediate solution, I don't want to crowd her, just be supportive. "What are you going to do?"

"That's just it. I don't know." She sniffles and blows out a breath. "She was so mad when I confronted her that she just walked away and refused to talk about it at all. I'm afraid if I keep pushing, I'll lose her. But I'm afraid if I don't push…" Her breath hitches.

"You'll lose her anyway," I finish for her.

She nods sadly and dabs at her eyes with a tissue. "See my dilemma?"

"She's what, eighteen?"

"Yeah. Just went off to college."

"So, she's a young adult. What about telling your parents? Surely, they can get involved or call the college. I bet they have protocols in place for situations like these."

Kiersten huffs a humorless laugh. "My parents believe that when you make dumb mistakes, you end up with the appropriate natural consequences. And basically, any mistake qualifies as being dumb in their eyes. I guarantee my mother would tell Nicole she wouldn't be in this situation if she had played harder to get."

"That doesn't even make sense."

"Not at all. But in her mind, if Nicole had waited and played the game, it would have given her time to see what kind of a man he really is before getting so deeply involved."

This thought process baffles me. "I don't even think that's true. An abusive man can manipulate things for a damn long time before showing his true colors. Even still, your mother would say that to an eighteen-year-old girl who is being beaten by her boyfriend?"

Kiersten scoffs, clearly no love lost between her and her mom. "You should hear the things she says to me. I almost never take Carson around her because she doesn't see a beautiful little boy. She sees a bad choice on my part, and I won't ever let him feel like he's a mistake. He's the best thing that ever happened to me. She's not going to sabotage his self-confidence because she has to be right."

Just hearing it second-hand makes me burn with rage for her. For them both. Here is this beautiful, hard working woman who always has a smile on her face and a beat in her hips, and her mother is still giving her grief over having a kid three years ago? It's no wonder she packed up and moved here. She has a better family dynamic amongst her friends.

I wish I knew how to help Kiersten with her sister, though. It's clear she's really torn up by the whole situation. Unfortunately, I've got no idea how to fix this for her. I don't even know where to start.

Before I can even try to help her come up with a solution, there's a knock at the door, and Tammy's head peaks in.

"Sorry to interrupt but we've got some new customers and y'all know better than to have me mix drinks."

I snicker. She's right. I tried teaching Tammy how to make a gin and tonic once. Even with only two ingredients, it didn't go well.

"I'll be right out."

She nods and quickly closes the door, leaving us to finish up.

Grabbing Kiersten's hand, I squeeze, ignoring the feel of her soft skin and the way she squeezes back. Now isn't the time for attraction. "Give yourself a few minutes and when you're ready, you can relieve me, okay?"

She smiles gratefully at me. It doesn't reach her eyes, but it's something. "Thanks, Paul. Again."

"Any time. I care about you."

She looks up at me from under her lashes and for a split second, I feel the chemistry between us. But again, there are bigger issues on the table right now. My job is to be a supportive boss, no matter how much I want to pull her into my arms and hug her.

Patting her leg, I leave her to her own thoughts and head back to the bar. Tammy is already popping the tops off some beer bottles so I know I probably have some orders to fill.

"What do you need?" I ask as I brush past her.

"One mojito and a dirty martini. Extra dirty with extra olives."

"On it."

First, though, I approach the lone man at the end of the bar who's glued to whatever game we have on the television. He catches my eye because of the biceps straining through his cotton t-shirt. I recognize an athlete when I see one. Probably pro, judging by his shoulder span. He can't be a Steer though. They're at training camp.

"Welcome to Frui Vita," I say as I approach and toss a

cocktail napkin down. "What can I get ya?"

He tears his eyes away from the screen. "I could go for a Jack and Coke. Hold the Coke."

I chuckle and pull the tumbler out, placing it on the napkin in front of him. "Neat or rocks?"

"Rocks, please."

I go about grabbing the ice and some small talk. Call me curious but I want to know how he ended up here. "Straight whiskey, huh? Rough night?"

"Nah. Just new to the area. I'm tired of being alone in my house and I got a recommendation to come check this place out and here I am."

Now he definitely has my attention. "Who in the world recommended our little place? We're kind of off the grid."

"Which is exactly what I was looking for." He takes a sip and nods his approval. "I asked my agent if he happened to know somewhere to hang out with low drama. I guess one of his other clients had told him about you."

"Hmm. Well, now you've piqued my curiosity. I'd love to know who is recommending us."

"Some guy named Heath is all I know."

"Heath Germaine?"

He thinks for a second as he lifts the glass to his mouth. "Sounds right. You know him?"

"A bit. He was here this weekend helping out with some projects for the low payment of beer and pizza." The guy chuckles because we've all been suckered into doing the heavy lifting for food and booze before. "He plays for the Steer. I take it you don't follow football."

"Not as much as I probably should, being that we're in Texas and all. I'm a hockey player. My time is spent on that more than anything."

Suddenly him being here makes more sense. He must

be starting with our hockey team, the San Antonio Slingers. I'll ask him at some point tonight but should let him get more comfortable with me first. Still, I'm glad to hear Heath is talking us up in his circle.

"Well, I'm Paul." I hold my hand out. He takes it and I can feel his forearm strength in his grip.

"Liam Tremblay."

"Liam, nice to meet you man. If you need another drink just let me know."

Liam raises his glass and goes back to watching the game.

It seems I'm going to owe Heath more than just a couple of drinks.

EIGHTEEN

Kiersten

I take a deep breath.

Then another.

And another.

I have been in full-on avoidance mode all day, but I have to leave for work soon and I'm running out of time.

I haven't talked to Nicole for a week. Seven days of her giving me one-word text replies and sending me straight to voicemail. It's so out of character for her and terrifies me. Not being able to hear her voice, to hear that she's okay makes me assume the worst. The scariest part is knowing "the worst" might be reality in this case, which is why I have to stop avoiding.

The last thing I want to do is call my mother, but she may be the only one who can help. I'm worried about Nicole and no, she doesn't live at home so maybe there's nothing my mother can do but maybe there is. Maybe she can talk some sense into my sister or call the police or, hell I don't know. I just know I'm out of my mind with worry and at a loss as to what to do. Spinning in circles isn't helping anything. At least this is an attempt to do something.

I take one last deep breath to steady my nerves and dial.

Three rings later, I'm about to hang up when she answers.

"Kiersten. Hello."

"Hi, mom."

"How are you? Is everything alright with you?"

"I'm fine. Why do you ask?"

"You don't ever seem to call me unless something is wrong. I just assumed."

I bite my tongue from reminding her that the phone works both ways, but it would inevitably end up with a lecture about being grateful for not being disowned and why I don't have a right to feel frustrated with the difficulties in my life. I am lying in the bed I made, after all. That's when I stopped calling to just touch base. I can't tell her all that, though. She doesn't understand how toxic she can be and will accuse me of being dramatic.

Instead, I play it safe. "Oh. Well, I guess there sort of is something concerning but I'm fine. Carson is, too, actually. Growing like a weed and finally done with his terrible two's."

"Don't get complacent too quickly. The trying three's are rapidly approaching."

He's actually already three, but I don't bother telling her she missed his birthday. It's unlikely she'll care, and for just this instant, we're not fighting. We're just a mom and daughter talking about the trials of parenthood.

And then my mother has to go and ruin the moment before it really even begins.

"Dealing with them all on your own is going to be terribly difficult. But I suppose that's to be expected when you're a single mother."

I bite back the retort I really want to say and opt for something a little tamer. "I may be single, but I'm not alone, Mom. I have an entire group of friends who love me and Carson and support us however they can."

She sighs dramatically. "It's not the same, Kiersten. A boy needs a father. You should have thought of that years ago."

"I did, Mom. But Spence died in a car accident, remember? That wasn't a choice any of us made."

"Such a shame that his family is hateful. The poor boy could have two sets of grandparents instead of only one that he doesn't even see very often anymore."

This conversation is beginning to piss me off. If I don't get it back on track, I may lose my cool and hang up. The only person that will hurt is my sister. So, I bite my tongue and rip the proverbial band-aid off.

"Anyway, I called because I'm worried about Nicole."

"Nicole? Why?" That catches her attention. But Nicole has always been her perfect baby. I don't begrudge my sister that. She's never let it go to her head. It's just a fact. "What's wrong with your sister?"

I hesitate only for a moment so I don't chicken out. "Have you met her boyfriend?"

"Jeremy? Of course. She's been dating him for over a year."

I shake my head in confusion. "A year? She told me they just started seeing each other."

Alarm bells go off in my brain. Nicole has been hiding this guy from me for months when I lived just around the corner from her. That tells me she knows in her gut that something is off and is afraid I'll make her see the truth. Now I'm even more scared for her safety.

"Oh pish," mom replies. "He spent Easter with us when you were at work. It's very serious. She even declined a scholarship to that fancy college in New York so they could go to school together and could continue dating."

She says all this wistfully, like my sister giving up her dreams, giving up a scholarship I didn't even know she had won, is this great thing. In the meantime, my heart is pounding at this new information. She's in so much deeper than I thought.

"I think it's very sweet. One of my babies might get married soon."

I ignore her dig, much more alarmed by this whole situation. "You know she came to visit me, right? Last weekend?"

"I didn't find out until after the fact when she finally told me you had invited her, but yes, I know she stayed with you for a couple of days. I also know you made her babysit while she was there to visit."

I ignore the obvious disapproval, completely unconcerned with her disdain right now. Suddenly, in light of everything happening with my sister, our rocky relationship seems trivial.

"Mom, Nicole had bruises on her arm. They looked like finger marks. And when I asked her about them, she got really defensive and mad at me for questioning her."

"What did she say they were from?"

"That's the thing. She came up with this weird excuse that she fell into an odd-shaped exercise machine at the gym. But I swear mom, it looked like someone had wrapped his hand around her bicep and squeezed, or maybe he shook her. I didn't see the other arm."

"Kiersten," she tsks. "If your sister says she fell, then

I'm inclined to believe her. I did not raise her to be a liar."

I tamp down my frustration, trying to get her to understand the severity of the situation. "But mom, have you seen her? She has these really dark circles under her eyes and she was kind of jumpy."

"You're worried because she hasn't been sleeping a lot her first semester away at college? Did *you* sleep a lot then? No. Because you were out with your friends having a good time on my dime."

"But—"

"No buts, Kiersten," she interrupts sternly. "I've known Jeremy for a long time. He comes from a lovely family and he's never been anything but sweet to Nicole. I will not allow you to accuse him of something when you haven't even met him."

"I—"

"Now, if that's all you called for, I need to know what size Carson is so I can buy him some quality clothes for his birthday present."

"Um, okay." I'm so stunned by her lack of concern for my sister's well-being. How can she dismiss the evidence so easily? I can't even think about clothing sizes at the moment. "Let me double-check all his tags and I'll let you know what he needs," I say quietly.

"Perfect."

Discouraged and disappointed, we say our goodbyes and hang up, and I sit back to think through the conversation.

Did I misread something? Am I blowing the whole situation out of proportion? I know what I saw, but maybe I'm being more dramatic than I thought.

Shaking my head, I push off the couch and head to the small bathroom. There's not one thing I know of that I can do to help my sister right now. The least I can do is get to work on time so I have a roof she can sleep under when the time comes. Because somehow, I know this isn't the end of the conversation, no matter what my mother thinks.

NINETEEN
Paul

As the humidity of summer tapers off a bit and the days solidly fall in the warm category versus hot, Kiersten slowly relaxes as well. The weight of the world seems to fall off her shoulders a bit. She's still worried—that much is clear—but when she mentions her sister finally answering her phone again, the sense of relief is also evident.

I'm glad for her, even though we both know this isn't over. Not by a long shot. But there's not a lot anyone can do until her sister is ready to get away from this guy. I think Kiersten is taking the time to prepare for that day. And I'm quietly supporting her, knowing I may have to cover her shifts or give her an advance when it finally comes time.

In the meantime, I can only assume word of mouth in the professional sports community is working because more and more athletes are showing up at the bar. Tammy is delighted to have more "young bucks" as she calls them, to dote on. Dwayne, on the other hand, is beside himself with the endless supply of people to challenge in a game of pool. I've never seen him this happy. And he's drinking less as he tries to keep his wits about him. I don't mind. My whole goal was to make customers happy here.

Speaking of, I'd like to thank Heath with a Sazerac or five, but he's not here tonight. Seems like he sent the rest of his team, though.

"Hey man. I hope it's okay that we all showed up." Frankie asks as I hand him a Dos Equis. "Apparently one of my teammates went to school with someone on the Slingers, you know the hockey team?"

I nod because who doesn't? They had a kick-ass season last year.

"When we decided to go out," he continues, "the Slingers were suddenly invited and now we're all here."

I try to play it cool, not wanting him to know exactly how excited I am by having so many patrons at one time. But I am. "The goal is to have a packed house, right? I just hope you guys enjoy yourselves."

"Okay cool. There weren't a lot of people here last time so we felt like we could let our hair down. We liked that. We need a place like that. It gets kind of annoying having to shake off groupies sometimes." Frankie rubs the back of his neck looking almost shy at admitting he needs a break from his fame every now and then. He doesn't need to be embarrassed around me, though. I may not have to worry about it, but I get it.

"That's why we put the tint up on the windows. Keeps things a little more private. And it's why I put up my new sign." I gesture to the large plaque against the wall that reads, *Keep Frui Vita a fun place to be. NO KINNEARING per management.*

Frankie inspects it, cocking his head to the side. "What's Kinnearing?"

Dammit. I knew no one would understand that part. But Kiersten swore it's a thing.

"It's like taking a picture of someone without their knowledge and posting it on the internet."

"Ooooh." Frankie nods slowly. "Nice. Thanks for that. I can't tell you the number of times people take the worst pics and post them just to get a laugh at our expense."

"Yeah, people can be dicks. But I don't want any of that here. I'll kick someone out first. Y'all just have a good time and relax. Let your boys know I'll be over in a second to take orders."

"Will do."

Frankie rejoins his group and I continue to hustle, pulling double duty. Kiersten is playing waitress today because Tammy's off, but she's late and hasn't called, which isn't like her. Normally it wouldn't bother me, but normally we wouldn't have a group of about twenty-five people here either.

They're all big guys, and they're all thirsty. I need to take some orders. Quickly, I finish up what I'm doing in the back end and head to their table.

"Hey, guys. Thanks for stopping in and my apologies for the wait," I greet. "Can I get you a round of beers or some shots?"

They start discussing drink options when someone says my name.

"Oh, hey Paul. Nice to see you, man."

I look up and recognize one of the guys at the table. He was here the other night. Apparently, he enjoyed the vibe like I was hoping he would.

"Glad you stopped in, Liam," I reply with a smile, quickly walking over for a handshake and fist bump. "I guess you decided this was a decent place to hang out."

"I did. Enjoyed myself the other night. Thought I'd come back. Maybe try out sitting at a table with people instead of the bar by myself."

"Whatever makes you comfortable. If you're happy, I'm happy."

"Have you met my teammates yet?"

"First time I've seen most of the guys here."

"Sure, sure. Since we'll be hanging out, let me introduce you to them."

He takes me around the table and I swear he introduces me to half the Slingers hockey team. When I've shaken hands and taken orders Liam pats me on the back. "I hope it's okay I brought so many people. I didn't realize you'd be on your own tonight."

The comment has me wondering where Kiersten is again. "I won't be for long. Seriously, the more the merrier. And listen, we don't have too many regulars but if anyone starts to harass you, just point out my new sign."

Liam cocks his head and furrows his brow. "What's Kinnearing?"

"You don't know either? Dammit. Kiersten swore up and down everyone would know it means taking pictures of people without their permission."

"Huh." He shrugs. "Maybe it's a chick thing."

"Well, considering Dwayne is the only non-athlete here tonight, and he doesn't even have a flip phone let alone Twitter, hopefully the sign is good enough. If for some reason it's not, you know where to find me."

Liam snickers. "I don't think we have to worry about Dwayne unless I try to take him on at pool again. He hustled me out of fifty bucks last time."

I can't help but laugh. "That's all on you, man. Any guy who spends this much time in a bar is a shark of some sort."

"Lesson learned."

"Anyway, let me get your drinks. No reason to keep y'all waiting anymore."

By this time, everyone's finally decided what they want, and taking orders is quick. Mostly it's buckets of ice-cold beer, keep 'em coming, which is easy for everyone. I go behind the bar to make drinks and that's when Kiersten rushes in, Carson in her arms.

"I'm sorry, Paul. I'm so sorry." She looks and sounds frazzled. "I totally forgot Lauren and Heath were going out of town so I don't have a babysitter. But don't worry, I got ahold of Jaxon and he's on his way to pick up Carson. It's just going to take about twenty minutes for him to get here…"

I hold my hands up. "Whoa, whoa, slow down." She stops talking. "Take a breath." She does. "It's okay. We only have the one big table and they're super cool. Plus, you're a good employee. I know this wasn't you being irresponsible. It's just a glitch. No biggie."

A weird expression crosses her face. "Really?"

"Yes really. Why do you look like that?"

"Like what?"

"Like you can't tell if I'm yanking your chain."

"Because most people say things like, 'These are the consequences of your actions, Kiersten,' or 'If you couldn't afford him, you shouldn't have had him, Kiersten.' I don't usually get a break."

Hearing her words shocks me. From what I've observed, Kiersten is responsible and tough. She's not a quitter. But she also has a soft look to her whenever she smiles at her son. How people outside her friend group aren't clamoring to help her out is beyond me.

"Maybe I'm not most people."

She bites her lip as relief crosses her face. "No, you're not." She says it quietly, like she's saying more than the words mean. "And thank you. I'll make it up to you, I promise. But let me get him settled real quick and I'll head to the back to grab some more supplies. Your stock of napkins is running low."

He glances to the shelf behind him. "Huh. I didn't even notice that."

She looks back at the guys who are already laughing and cutting up. "Seems like you've had your hands full. I'll go get more in just a second."

Hauling Carson and a bag full of stuff to the side, she pulls out a tiny little portable chair and sets it in a quiet corner where we can see him, but he's not behind the bar. Then she hands him a tablet. "Stay here. Don't move."

The squeal and kick of his legs indicate he's more than excited to have the device and I have no doubt he'll be fine until Jaxon gets here.

I come around the bar and she helps me set some buckets on the tables that have been pushed together for everyone to fit. Once we're satisfied they're all set, I think about those napkins again.

"Why don't you go set your stuff down in the back and grab those napkins."

She looks at Carson nervously.

"I'll watch him while you grab the stuff," I promise. "All I'm doing is slinging beers so I'm facing him the whole time."

She nods and gives me that smile I like so much. "Thanks," she says and puts her hand on my arm. A jolt of electricity buzzes through me and I know what that is. Attraction. Attraction I shouldn't have but why wouldn't

I? Kiersten is the whole package and she's getting harder to resist every day. "I'll be right back." Turning to her son she calls, "Don't move, Carson."

He ignores her, engrossed in whatever he's watching.

Getting back to work, I busy myself finishing up some specialty drinks. It only takes a couple of minutes so as soon as they're delivered, I look up and realize Carson is gone.

My heart beating wildly, I look around frantically, praying he didn't accidentally walk out the front door. I would have heard that, right? The door opening? And how did a three-year-old go missing in a matter of seconds? And how did I accomplish that the one and only time Kiersten needed me for something?

All these throughs run through my brain as I scan the room before finding him just feet from where he started— by the table full of men, staring at one of the players.

Rushing over, mostly to calm my own nerves and not because anything is wrong, I squat down in front of him. "Whatcha doing, little man?"

At that moment, Liam turns from his conversation and sees the little boy. His face lights up. "Hey there. Who are you?"

Carson scowls. "You no Unca Heat."

Liam looks over at me, brows furrowed. "Uhh, can you translate that for me? I don't speak toddler."

"Say that again Carson?"

"He no Unca Heat."

"He's not… oh! No, he's not Uncle Heath. But he's sort of his friend." I look back up at Liam, feeling like an introduction is in order. "This is Carson, Heath Germaine's nephew."

"I never would have put that together. I wonder if

Shawn knows this guy. I think they were friends in college or something. Hey Shawn!" Liam yells over the table making his teammate cut his conversation short to answer. "You're friends with Heath Germain, right?"

"Yeah. What's up?"

"You know this little dude?" He points down at Carson. "This is Heath's nephew."

"No shit?" Shawn glances over the table and down at the toddler. "You definitely didn't get your looks from your uncle, kid. You're way better looking."

"My Unca Heat. Gimme tashe." Carson points at the table and we all look around, completely dumbfounded as we try to figure out what baby talk means.

"Uhhh… what was that?" I ask Carson who sighs deeply, like we're the ones making this hard.

"Gimme. Tashe."

"Oh, *trash*." Liam seems to have a lightbulb moment, thank God because this could have gone on for a while. "You want to help. Here ya go." He picks up a used napkin and rolls it into a ball before handing it to Carson. "Here's my trash. Go throw it in that trashcan right over there."

Carson happily runs away, tossing his *tashe* away and coming back for more. Liam grabs another used napkin and hands it right over.

"You don't have to do that. I can clear the table off for you if it's too cluttered."

"No way. I know what's about to happen." Carson takes off across the room again and I make a note to empty that bin soon. "My nephew was on self-imposed trash duty for a year at that age. Don't take one thing off this table. I'm preparing myself to keep Carson entertained for a while."

I have to admit, the man is a genius.

Kiersten comes into the room, carrying a box full of

napkins. I hustle over to her, taking it out of her arms and putting it back behind the bar until we can get to it.

"How'd it go?" she asks, looking around. "He okay?" Her eyes finally find him as he darts back and forth from the table to the trash can. Her chin drops to her chest before looking back up at me knowingly. "He put himself on trash duty, didn't he?"

"Now where were you when we needed a translator?" I ask with a chuckle.

"I'm sorry he's bothering everyone. I'll get him situated with his tablet again."

I grab her arm to stop her. "Leave him alone. He's happy and he's entertaining the guys."

"The guys?" she asks with amusement.

"*The guys* on Heath's football team and apparently *the guys* on the Slinger's hockey team, too. They seem solid and they're enjoying Carson."

We look over just as Shawn lifts Carson up and tips him over so he can reach for something in the middle of the table. When he sets him back down on the floor, they go in for a fist bump before Carson takes off running again.

Kiersten's lips quirk up. "Well, he is a good trash man."

"That he is."

Now that that's settled, we ease back into our routine, working around each other as we chat.

"Jaxon will be here soon, hopefully. I'm not in the mood to hear *Sweet Home Alabama* quoted to me all night long even though I'm sure it's coming."

"Never saw it."

She stops and stares at me. "What? It's right up your alley. Reese Witherspoon and that guy whose name I can never remember."

"I remind you of a non-memorable guy in a romantic

comedy? I need to up my game," I joke.

"He's a small business owner and has rugged good looks," she replies. "Plus, there is the famous line… *you have a baby? In a bar?*" She tosses in a thick Southern accent that I assume is character based.

"Ah. Now I see the connection."

Kiersten's phone rings and she glances down at it, her face immediately falling. "Oh no." Looking back up at me she asks, "Do you mind? It's Jaxon."

"Go ahead. It's important if he's calling."

As she answers, she scrunches her nose and reaches up to dig her fingers in her hair. I try really hard not to notice what the movement does to her breasts but to no avail. Judging by the looks on some of the guy's faces across the room, I'm not the only one whose attention she caught. I narrow my eyes in their direction, but they don't see me.

"Hello? Hey." Her head drops and I know it's bad news. "No, it's okay. It's not your responsibility. I just screwed up this time. It happens. Yeah. Seriously Jaxon. Stop apologizing. Okay. Yeah. Okay. See ya."

She hangs and up and sighs, avoiding my gaze and trying to fight back tears.

"Jaxon got stuck at school. He thought he was done but it's going to be a couple more hours. I'm sorry, Paul. I can't believe I screwed up this much."

"Kiersten, stop."

"I just hate leaving you in a lurch but we both know I can't keep Carson here with me all night."

"Kiersten, I'm not mad."

She blinks back the tears. "You aren't?"

"No. You're never late. You never call in. If anything, it's about time you stopped putting the rest of us to shame," I joke.

Her lips quirk up, but not quite into a smile. Knowing her, she's probably not just embarrassed, she's probably crunching numbers in her head on what she can cut back on if she doesn't work tonight. Which gives me an idea. It's probably crossing the line, but right now I can't find it in me to care.

"You know I live in the back, right? In the apartment?"

She furrows her brow briefly as she watches Carson make yet another trash run. "Yeah."

"Why don't I call Tammy in to cover me and I'll take him to my place when she gets here?"

A mixture of emotions crosses Kiersten's face—relief, confusion, resolve, and finally denial.

"That's really nice of you Paul, but I can't ask you to do that."

"You're not asking."

"I know. But it's Tammy's day off."

"And just yesterday she was asking if I needed her tonight because her husband is working," I interject. "You know how much she hates to be home alone."

She nods. We've both heard it many times before. There's nothing Tammy hates more than an empty house and nothing to do.

"But you're my boss," Kiersten says, not able to let it go. "Don't you think it would be weird to be watching one of your employees' kids?"

I shrug because I don't actually find it weird at all. "We're a small business, Kiersten, not a corporation. Things are different here. It's no stranger than all your friends showing up to do renovations."

"I think they showed up for the pizza, beer, and sledge-hammers."

"No. They *stayed* for the pizza, beer, and sledgehammers. They *showed up* because it was the friendly thing to do."

She worries her lip trying to decide if she wants to trust me with her child. I get it. Not everyone is safe these days. But I'm one of the good guys and right now I want to make her feel like she's not alone. Like she has an extended army of people to help her when she needs it. "If it makes you feel better, I have a mountain of paperwork I need to knock out. We'll go to the apartment, put on some cartoons, and when Carson knocks out on the couch, I'll get some work done away from the office where I can concentrate better anyway."

Still fidgeting with her phone, she looks up at me, decision made. "Are you sure? I mean, look at him." Carson runs by with a straw wrapper in his hands. "He could do this all night."

"So, all the trash in my apartment will be picked up. Sounds like a sweet deal."

She cocks an eyebrow at me.

"I'm kidding Kiersten. We'll be fine. I'll take you back with us and show you around so you can point out anything I might need to put up high really quick. You'll just be out here. We'll be close enough you can check in on us, or I can come grab you if we need you."

She sighs and I'm almost positive it's with relief, although there may be a bit of resignation mixed in.

"Fine. Okay. I will gratefully take you up on this offer, but only if Tammy agrees," she tacks on quickly. "Once he falls asleep, he'll be fine, but promise me you'll come get me if you need anything."

"We'll be fine, Kiersten. I promise. He's three. How hard could he be?"

TWENTY

Kiersten

"*How hard could he be?*"

If only Paul knew how many times I've regretted saying those words, he would have refrained from uttering them. Instead, he basically jinxed himself. Now I'm almost afraid to go back to his apartment to check on the boys.

When Paul initially offered to watch Carson for me, I was hesitant at best. Not because I don't trust Paul. He's never been anything but kind and Jaxon has raved about him for years. It wasn't a safety or trust issue. It was more about allowing myself to cross that line.

It's no secret that I have a crush on my boss. Lauren won't let it go and keeps pushing me to do something about it. And Heath—he's never said he knows, but he certainly finds ways to harass me about it.

I still don't know where my feelings came from. Maybe it's just admiration that morphed into something more real. Or maybe it's genuine attraction.

Either way, I knew the second I accepted his offer of

watching my son that that would be it. The crush would get even deeper and my chances of heartache would get more significant. And yet, I did it anyway. Only a few hours later and I already know my hunch was right.

I'm in trouble. Big trouble. My feelings continue to grow and they're not going away any time soon. But honestly, how could I not find Paul attractive? The way he treated me when I was late and didn't have a babysitter—the way he treated Carson as he put himself on trash duty—quite frankly, it was swoon-worthy. And I've never used the word "swoon-worthy" before.

Double-checking that the doors are all locked, I flip the last of the lights off in the front. It was a busy night, but a lot of fun. It's wild how fast Heath's recommendation to his friends brought in new customers, but that's exactly what we've all been hoping for. I almost got teary closing out the till when I realized we'd pulled in more in one night than we did all last week. That's not including tips. I thought Tammy was going to fall over when she calculated how much cash she was taking home.

All in all, it was a fantastic night. I'm hoping Paul's night was just as exciting.

Actually no. I hope his night was boring and calm, but I don't have high hopes.

Winding my way around the back hallway, I slowly open the door marked "private residence," hoping not to disturb anyone who may be sleeping. The apartment is nice, if not a little on the small side. I'd best describe it as an efficiency, except there's a partial wall separating the bedroom area from the rest of the place. It doesn't leave much of a sound barrier when trying to be quiet in the middle of the night.

Peeking in, I see Paul sitting upright, head rested

against the back of the couch, snoring lightly. Carson's head is on his lap, his baby lips slightly open as he breathes deeply.

And now I'm swooning again.

They look so precious together, I can't help but document this moment. If I'm going to melt into a puddle, Tammy can fan her cheeks right along with me later. That's my justification for snapping a quick picture, whether I'm lying to myself or not.

Taking an extra moment to just watch them, I thank my lucky stars for once again putting people in my life that give my son the care he deserves. Funny how I was angry Spence's family essentially drove us out of town a few months ago, and yet it ended up being the best thing that could have happened to us.

I creep over to the couch and put a hand on Paul's shoulder, shaking gently.

"Paul," I whisper. "I'm back."

He lifts his head, eyes slowly opening. It takes a second for him to register what's happening, but he eventually comes to.

"Hey," he says quietly rubbing the heel of his hand in his eye. "How did it go?"

"I should be asking you the same thing," I say with a small chuckle. "Looks like he wore you out."

Paul strokes Carson's hair gently and there go the butterflies in my stomach again, fluttering all around.

"I vastly underestimated how long this kid can stay awake. He spent most of the night running circles around the island in the kitchen."

"I should have warned you about that. That's his go-to move when he's overly tired. But it looks like you eventually got him to sleep."

"Or he eventually got me to sleep. Could go either way." Paul sits up a little, careful not to jostle Carson too much. "What time is it anyway?"

"Close to four."

His eyes widen. "Holy shit. Was it that busy? Why didn't you come get me?"

"Relax. We only had a few more customers come in after you left. Tammy and I just wanted to make sure the till was balanced correctly so we did it twice. It was… a lot different than normal."

I can see the gears turning in Paul's head as he mulls over my words. I'm thrilled to deliver such good news to him, I'm just not sure he's fully comprehending it in his sleepy state.

As Paul carefully stands up, I realize we can have this conversation later. It's time for us to go. Daylight will come soon and we have an appointment. I reach out to pick up my son but Paul beats me to it. "I got him."

"It's okay. I don't want you to have to walk through the parking lot barefoot."

"I'm not going to the parking lot," he whispers and carefully pulls Carson to his chest. He snuggles right into Paul's large frame, barely waking up enough to lick his pouty lips. It warms my heart to see my son feeling comfortable. It also makes me long to give him a daddy. "You guys are staying here tonight after we talk about that till. He'll never go back to sleep otherwise."

I'm too stunned to argue with him as he carries Carson into the bedroom, especially since he's right about my son's sleep habits. It's one of the reasons Carson stays over at Lauren's so much.

While I wait, I plop down on the couch and begin cleaning up the mess my little tornado of a child left in his wake. I'm wiped from a long night, but it usually takes my brain a couple of hours to settle enough to finally sleep anyway. If Paul wants more information, I have enough energy left to give it to him.

He's back quickly and sits on the edge of the small coffee table so we're facing each other. His hair is sticking up and his stubble has grown in, his eyes still a little groggy from sleep. God, he's sexy. He's also my boss who just did me a huge favor. *Down girl.*

"Thank you again for watching Carson. I never meant to put you in a bind."

He shakes his head slowly and I swear I see heat behind his eyes. "It's never an inconvenience when you care about the person you're helping."

He grabs my hand and interlaces our fingers, the heat of his palm both burning my skin and soothing the ache of loneliness in my body. It's been so long since someone touched me like this, without needing something from me, just to show affection. It confuses me. I know Paul is attracted to me, but he's made it clear there can never be anything between us except friendship.

I should pull away, but I don't want to.

"You amaze me, Kiersten," Paul says quietly, his eyes boring into mine. "You carry so much on your shoulders, and yet you always have a smile on your face."

"If I don't smile, I might cry."

"That's what I mean. I admire your determination and strength. And you're raising such an amazing little boy. I've never met anyone like you."

"I've never met anyone like you either," I admit quietly. "Who cares deeply about the people around him and wants to make them feel cared for. Even just the simple things like adding a house rule about pictures to your business."

"Nah. That's about keeping my customers happy so I can make money."

I shake my head because he's wrong. "No, that's you sacrificing the easy marketing route of hashtags and social media so people who have limited options have a place to be."

"You make me sound like a saint working with the disadvantaged."

"And you make it sound like you don't understand that having a job where a camera is in your face all the time doesn't mean you don't deserve anonymity sometimes, but you do."

His thumb runs over the top of my hand as he quiets, mulling over my words. Maybe I'm biased because I'm friends with Heath and I know how vicious people can be online, but having a welcoming place to be is a treat. I don't understand how Paul doesn't see what a kind thing he's doing. It's as if his own humility trumps his ability to see himself completely. I know he thinks he's making decisions specifically to grow a new business, but I personally think that's why it took so long for him to put together a business plan. He had to find the right need first.

"Well," he says, his eyes locked on the movement of his thumb. "Either way, I appreciate all your hard work."

"Like you said earlier, it's never an inconvenience when you care about the person you're helping."

His eyes snap up to meet mine and there's something new in his eyes. Part question. Part resolve. Lots of heat.

"Kiersten." He says my name quietly, his body beginning to slowly lean in.

"Yes?" My body responds, moving just as slowly, knowing he's not going to stop again.

"Tell me you don't want this." It's a beg. It's a plea. It's an understanding that if we cross this line there's no going back.

But I can't give him the answer he wants. Or maybe I give him the exact answer he wants. I'm as unsure as he is. The only thing I know is if tonight is all I get, I'll take it. "I can't say that because it wouldn't be true."

And then his lips are on mine. Firm and warm, exploring and tasting. When his tongue finally invades my mouth, there's no stopping the frenzy that begins.

I climb onto Paul's lap, thrusting my fingers into his hair and pulling him close. His arms wrap around my waist and we both groan when he presses me down harder on his straining erection. It only lasts a second before he resituates us on the couch, me on my back, him nestled between my legs as he grinds and mimicks the motion of his tongue.

Suddenly he pulls back, eyebrows drawing together. "Birth control?"

"IUD," I answer and his body immediately slumps with relief just before he kisses me again, our movements taking on a desperation now that we both know what's coming.

My hands leave his hair and push under his shirt, desperate to feel his warm skin. I run my hands over the muscles of his hard back, loving the feel of them flexing as he moves.

"Please take this off," I beg, pushing at the material until he sits up long enough to pull it over his head and toss it on the floor.

He gazes down at me and I'm sucker punched with emotion. It's been so long since someone has looked at me like I'm the most beautiful thing in the world. So long since fingertips have grazed my skin and lips have made their way back down to nip at my neck. So long since I've been looked at like a woman worthy of reverence. I've never been worshiped like this by a man who was willing to wait months as he got to know me. My lips part as the gravity of this moment hits me.

"I've had dreams about this," Paul whispers as he places gentle kisses down to my collarbone. "You, underneath me, your long legs wrapped around me."

"I've had the same dreams," I admit, running my fingers through his hair again, holding him close. "Why didn't you do anything about it?"

He pulls back just enough to make eye contact. "I never want you to feel like I'm taking advantage of you. I'm your boss but that doesn't mean you don't hold the power. If this isn't something you want, just say the word."

I pull his mouth back to mine and answer him with my kiss.

We take our time removing each other's clothing and exploring the skin we find underneath. Paul is lean and muscular. Not bulky like the friends in my life, but strong from hard work and manual labor. He's gentle and reverent, as only a man who has experience can be, worshiping every inch of my body. When he nips at the inside of my elbow, I gasp.

"Did I just find a sensitive spot?" he asks with an amused chuckle before biting gently at it again.

I gasp for the second time. "I didn't know that was there. No one's ever kissed me so thoroughly."

A growl rumbles up from his throat. "Their loss. You taste like honey."

I can't help the small giggle that bursts out of me. "You mean I taste like hops. I've been slinging drinks all night."

"Semantics."

There's no more talking after that. No words are necessary as I run my hands over his skin, and he tastes my nipples. When we're fully naked and he finally hooks one of my knees over his arm and pushes into me, it feels like coming home.

The thought is fleeting as we push and pull, groan and moan, thrust and grind, taking from each other and giving just as much in return. And when we reach our climax together, I know I'm ruined for anyone else. No one will ever make me feel this way—loved, cared for, desired.

Coming down from the high, our breathing evening out, Paul pulls out of me slowly and settles me on his lap. His gentle kisses are exactly what my battered heart needs in this moment. There will never be another man who makes me feel like Paul does. My boss, my friend, my lover—he's it for me. He's it for *us*.

"Why don't you sleep in my bed tonight?"

I pull back to look at his handsome face, wishing he could come snuggle with me, but knowing it wouldn't be appropriate with Carson in that same bed. I nod in agreement, even though my heart wants to stay right here on the couch with him.

"Thank you."

"I should be saying the same to you."

Smiling shyly, he leans in and takes my lips one more time. It's a goodnight kiss, but I hope it's also the beginning of something more.

I finally push off his lap and grab my shirt off the floor, throwing it and my panties on quickly before heading toward bed.

Turning as I enter the room, I look back at him. "You're a really amazing man, Paul."

He stops getting dressed as I speak, hopefully absorbing the words I can't seem to stop from saying.

"And not just because of your bedroom skills. But just because you're you. Anyway… goodnight."

"Goodnight Kiersten."

I don't look back this time, having said everything I needed to say. Instead, I climb onto the mattress and snuggle next to my son. The bed smells like musk and detergent and man. It's going to be hard to fall asleep surrounded by the scent of the one I like so much.

Until suddenly, I just drift.

TWENTY-ONE
Paul

It's been five hours since I was inside Kiersten and I can't stop thinking about it. It was… *she* was more than I ever imagined. Feeling her skin on mine, the gentle thrum of her pulse under my lips when I kissed her neck, her slickness as I thrust in and out of her—it's a memory I want to keep in the forefront of my mind. I don't remember ever feeling so complete. Like I was home. But that's how she made me feel. Truthfully, it's how she always makes me feel, it was just on a much larger scale when we were naked.

I had no intention of jumping Kiersten last night. I tried to stay solidly within the boundaries I had set, but when she woke me up, looking a little rough around the edges from a long night of work, I couldn't stop myself. Honestly, I didn't want to. She was so beautiful and so excited for the bar's success, it was easy to get caught up in the moment. Or maybe that's just my excuse to myself.

The most difficult part of it all is, I like Kiersten. And I'm not even sure *like* is the right word for how I feel.

Kiersten is the total package of everything I've always wanted in a woman. She's smart and witty and charming. She's beautiful on and off the dance floor. But she doesn't come alone. She's a package deal, kind of like I am. The difference is I come with a floundering business while she comes with an amazing child, and neither of those things is complimentary to the other.

That child is why I offered for Kiersten to stay over. I really was worried he'd wake up and refuse to go back to sleep. In hindsight, maybe I should have thought about the morning after. I hope it isn't going to be awkward. We probably need to have a hard conversation to make sure we're both on the same page. That page being it can never happen again.

And Carson will probably be hungry during that talk, so pancakes it is. Well, that and because he's just a great kid. Babysitting was more fun than I thought it would be. Carson has a wicked sense of humor for a three-year-old and I found myself laughing a lot at his antics. He also has more energy than I expected. After watching him throw away trash for a solid half-hour, I should have figured he'd keep going until he dropped.

I'm in the middle of making a batch when Carson comes running into the room yelling, "Paw! Paw?"

He obviously can't see me from the other side of the island, but I can see him, standing still and looking around. It's amusing to watch him listen for some clue as to where I am when all he has to do is look up to see me.

"Paw?" he yells again, only this time Kiersten is behind him trying to shush him so I finally give.

"I'm right here, buddy."

Finally looking in the right direction, Carson sees me, his eyes lighting up as he yells, "Paw!" and runs over to hug my leg. It's weird how that one simple act makes a jolt of happiness run through me. No wonder everyone loves this kid so much. Baby hugs automatically make you feel happy.

Kiersten meanders in behind him with her bed head and smudged makeup. Damn she's beautiful. I wish life circumstances were different. But failure isn't an option and that's what will happen if we continue with this romance and it's not just me who stands to lose a lot.

"What are you doing?"

"Making breakfast. I figured this guy…" I pick Carson up and squeeze his side making him giggle, "would be hungry and this is the only thing I really know how to make that doesn't require a deep fryer or grill."

"That's really thoughtful of you, thank you." Kiersten settles on one of the small stools in front of me. "Did you sleep okay? I feel bad you got the couch."

"Nah. It was no big deal. I've slept on the couch in the office more times than I can count. This was still better."

She grimaces. "That lumpy old thing that smells like socks?"

I scoff. "It doesn't smell that bad."

"You may need to get those olfactory senses checked out because yes, yes it does. Why do you think I always opt for the plastic chair?"

I think back to the multiple times she, Tammy, and even my former bartender Desiree have been in my office and she's right—they never sit on the couch.

"And here I thought you were just a hard worker and didn't want to get too comfortable."

"Yes. Yes, that's exactly what I meant. Hard worker. Mm-hmm." She smirks and I can't help how much I enjoy having this small moment together. Her, rumpled from sleep. Me, dutifully making breakfast. Carson, hard at work with a puzzle. For the first time maybe ever, I can see this for my future and I want it. I want it so much it scares me.

"Since Carson is entertained and I'm still making breakfast, why don't you go get cleaned up?" I point to a box in the corner with the spatula I'm holding. "There are a bunch of extra work shirts in there if you want to grab one. I don't think I have any shorts that'll fit you but at least you'll have a clean shirt."

"Thanks, Paul." She begins riffling through the box, presumably to find her size. I wish I had my own oversized shirts in there. Seeing her in nothing but a giant-sized t-shirt would be quite the sight to see. Instead, I remind myself what happened last night was a one-time thing. I don't have the right to see her intimately now that the moment has passed.

Flipping her hair around to get it out of her face, Kiersten continues with her dig. "I can't imagine how I must look since I didn't shower before bed."

"You look beautiful."

The words are out of my mouth before I can stop them. A blush covers Kiersten's face and I want to kick myself for making things awkward. They were starting out so well.

She clears her throat and sets the box aside. "I'm uh…" she gestures over her shoulder with her thumb. "Just gonna shower."

"Take your time. Extra towels are under the sink."

She nods and turns to Carson, kissing him on top of the head before disappearing into the small bathroom.

It only takes a couple of minutes to finish making pancakes. Unfortunately, I only have the counter to sit at, and

I don't want Carson to fall off a barstool. Coffee table it is.

I bring two plates, one for each of us, and settle on the floor, stretching out my legs in front of me. Carson immediately climbs onto my lap like he's known me forever. Truthfully, I feel the same way. There's just something about this kid that draws me in and makes me want to take care of him all the time.

Kissing him on the top of the head, I can't help feeling bad his dad and grandparents are missing this. I know those people are major assholes, but they truly are the losers in this situation.

I mean, who wouldn't enjoy trying to get this kid dressed and watching him run around with some Paw Patrol underwear on his head before I can finally wrangle him into his clothes? I am quickly learning there is not a dull moment with this kid around.

"Oh, wow. You got dressed, buddy?"

I run my fingers through my probably disheveled hair and huff a deep breath. "That was more exercise than I've done in a while. Good thing he had more than one pair of clean underwear in that bag. He wore the first pair on his head while I got him changed."

Kiersten smirks and begins picking up the dirty clothes I haven't gotten to yet. "He thinks it's funny."

"Oh, it was. I just didn't want a naked baby butt all over my couch. I had my head there last night and probably will again at some point."

She giggles and once again I'm hit with how much I wish this was our morning normal.

"There's more pancakes on the counter if you're hungry."

"I appreciate it but we actually have an appointment this morning." She zips the bag closed and begins gathering puzzle pieces. "I know you do direct deposits for us but do you happen to have a paycheck stub? Or the last two?"

I furrow my brow at the odd request. "Yeah sure. They're in the office. Everything okay?"

She smiles brightly and nods. "Fine. Carson has a WIC appointment this morning and I need proof of income."

"What's WIC?" I feel like I've heard of it before but I never really paid attention.

"It's just a program that provides a small amount of food for Carson. Milk, cheese, eggs, things like that."

I can feel my hackles rise. I had no idea things were that bad for them financially. "Are you okay?" I immediately ask. "Do you need money for food? You work so hard, I'm more than happy to help."

Her chin drops as she fights to keep a smile off her face, cheeks pinkening. I already know she's about to turn me down. "No, really. We're okay. Our situation isn't unusual. Lots of single moms get WIC to help supplement. It's just the way it goes sometimes."

"Oh man Kiersten, I'm sorry."

"It's fine. My story is mild compared to some of them. You'd be shocked what some single moms go through trying to provide for their kids. I have a great job and great friends. And I have you."

I break away my gaze, clearing my throat. We need to have this conversation, I just hate that it has to happen at all. "Um, about last night."

She holds her hand up to stop me. "It's okay. I know it was… unexpected. I don't plan to start telling everyone or whatever. That would be weird at work. Plus, I don't even know what this is anymore."

The look on her face is so hopeful. I can't string her along. I can't make her think we can be anything more than what we are. Instead, I blurt out the first words that come to my head.

"Kiersten, I'm not interested in dating you."

As soon as the words are out of my mouth, I know I've made a mistake. It's not at all how I feel, but even worse, it looks like I've just slapped her. I grimace. "Dammit, that's not what I mean."

She blinks a few times. "Well, what do you mean?"

I try to come up with a way to explain everything I feel about her and why it grieves me to have only one night together. But how do I put the depth of what I feel into words? How can I possibly explain how much is on the line should it all go wrong? I have to try, though.

"You're my employee." She narrows her eyes at my shoddy explanation so I keep going. "Crossing those boundaries reflects badly on my business. It reflects badly on me. At some point, it could reflect badly on you, too. I don't want to hurt any of us."

Her chest heaves as she visibly tries to quell her anger. "Maybe you should have thought of that before you offered to babysit my son and brought him into this mess."

"That's different." I scramble to my feet, hoping to diffuse the situation. I knew my honesty would hurt, but I don't think I'm expressing myself in the right way either. I don't think she's understanding my motivation isn't about her. It's about protecting all of us.

"How?" She throws her arms out in frustration. "How is you building a relationship with the son of a single mom different? It could still lead to boundary issues, right? Hell, he's already attached to you. You don't think that's a problem?"

I hang my head. She's right. "Shit Kiersten, I'm sorry. I don't mean it to sound like I'm rejecting you or him. I'm not. I like both of you, so much. And I wish it could be different. But it can't."

Failure is not an option.

She takes a calming breath before speaking again. "Paul, I like you. Too much, probably. I like the way you run your bar. I like the way you take care of people. But this," she points back and forth between the two of us, and then between Carson and I. "This isn't okay. I won't be anyone's side piece when you're in the mood and I won't be a dirty little secret. And I certainly won't make him a dirty little secret. Ever."

My eyes widen in shock. "That's not—"

She holds up her hand again and I stop, knowing it's probably better to hold my tongue until I can figure out the right words to say.

"Come on, sweet boy." She grabs the bag and tosses the strap over her shoulder. "We have to go play."

"Go pay?" Carson asks, looking up from the last of his breakfast.

"Yep." She says it with a smile, but I can see the hurt in her eyes still. I put that there and I don't know how to make it go away. "Say thank you to Paul so we can go."

"Tanku, Paw." He gives me another hug around the legs and my heart squeezes like there's a vice around it as I rub his back.

"Any time, buddy."

Then Kiersten takes him by the hand and doesn't look back.

TWENTY-TWO

Kiersten

The last thing I want to do is go to the WIC office. I know it's nothing to be embarrassed about. We all need help sometimes and I've paid into the system for years. Forty dollars in food a month for a couple of years won't even make a dent in the taxes I've had taken out of my paychecks. I'm just not really in the emotional headspace to keep my chin up this morning. Getting only a couple of hours sleep isn't helping either.

This appointment is not about me, though. It's not about Paul or the one night we had together or the shitty way he talked to me this morning. It's not even about the fact that I know I misunderstood what he was trying to say and let my own insecurities stop us from having an adult conversation. I'll have to fix that later. But first, this appointment is about Carson and it would serve me well to keep that at the forefront of my mind for at least a little while.

Looking down at him as we walk along the sidewalk, I gently remind my son about how to behave at appointments like these. If my mother taught me anything of value, it's that we want to be respectful of the fact that this is someone's workplace.

"When we're inside, I want you to be very quiet, Carson." I put my finger over my lips to reiterate what I'm telling him.

"Be kiat?"

"Yep. No yelling. And stay with mommy the whole time."

We walk in the non-descript front door into an equally non-descript room. It's like any other government office I've ever been in—plain cream paint with posters about nutrition and breastfeeding on the walls, blue plastic chairs, a long desk separating the staff from those of us waiting. It does have one thing going for it though—a giant wooden toy block. I'm sure it's sticky from years of little kids playing with it, but I don't mind as long as Carson is entertained. And from the way his eyes light up when he sees it, I'm sure he'll be happy for a while.

"I pay, mommy."

"Go ahead, buddy," I encourage since it's just a few short feet from where I have to check-in.

I smile politely at the staff member I'm approaching. I'm sure working in community service is draining. There's an element of customer service that goes with it, just like my job. I'd rather not be the customer that makes her day more difficult.

"Hi, I have an appointment." She doesn't look up from her computer, clicking away on the keys.

"Name?"

"Kiersten Willoughby."

"Child's name?"

"Carson. Same last name."

It takes her only a few seconds to pull up my information and finally make eye contact, although she still appears really bored. I feel bad for her. It's still morning and the workday isn't even halfway over. Things are not going to go well if it's already this draining on her mood.

"I need a utility bill, proof of income, and your child's shot record," she finally says and I hand over what I have, which isn't much.

"Um, my boss couldn't give me any paycheck stubs because he does it all online." I hate that I can hear the embarrassment in my voice, but she's not giving me good vibes. "Is there a way I can email them to you to print? I'm sorry," I tack on quickly, feeling bad that I didn't stop to think long enough during my conversation with Paul to get what I need at work.

She sighs and hands me a business card with the email address on it. "Have a seat and just come back up when you're done."

I thank her and sit down in the closest chair, making quick work of screenshotting my proof and emailing it to her, while she checks in someone else who actually brought the right paperwork. Getting back in line, I try to stop mentally berating myself for my lack of preparation but it's hard. Very little sleep, a humiliating conversation, and humbling myself to get food for my son isn't a good combination.

When I get back to the front of the line, I smile again. She gives me no reaction, except to look at her monitor. I wait patiently, hoping she's looking for my email and not just ignoring me.

"You only have two paycheck stubs."

I furrow my brow. "That's all the paper said I needed."

"It's better to have three."

"Do you need me to send you another one?"

She sighs and rolls her eyes as if I'm causing her tremendous grief. "We'll make do."

An idea hits me that will hopefully make this process easier. "Um, will last year's tax return help?"

"Probably. Let's see it." I hand it over to her, grateful I had the foresight to have it with me, until she huffs her frustration again. "Where's the rest of it?"

"What do you mean? That's it."

She holds it up to show me, like I don't know what I just handed her. "This is just the first two pages."

"That's what the WIC paper said I needed to bring."

"No. We need your adjusted gross income."

"It's right there." I point out the line that is clearly labeled "adjusted gross income."

"Well, that's not what we need."

Feeling frazzled and confused, I don't want to argue with her, but this isn't the first time I've done this. It's also not the first time someone has tried to make me feel like shit for being here. "The first two pages is exactly what the office we used to go to has taken every year for the last two years."

She turns to her co-worker who has obviously been listening but stayed silent for this whole exchange. "Can you pull up her previous account?" I wait quietly, biting my lip to keep the tears at bay. Standing behind the co-worker, she finally points at the monitor. "See that's what we need. Open it up." She suddenly looks confused. "Why don't they have the rest of it? That's just the first two pages. I hate when people don't know what they're doing."

I blink a few times, trying hard not to cry. People are staring at me and she's talking about my lack of income in front of all these people. I haven't felt this humiliated since

Spence's mother paid me off to go away. Like we're unimportant and not worth being treated like human beings.

She turns to another woman who I assume is a manager, although why she hasn't gotten involved yet is a bit baffling. "Can you look at this? She's saying this is all she needs but there should be more pages."

On top of my humiliation, I'm starting to get angry as well. This isn't right. I've followed all the instructions. I've brought everything they said they needed. They're even looking in my previous account to prove I'm not trying to scam the system and she's still treating me like I'm a criminal for forty dollars in food.

"Have a seat," she says over her shoulder. "We'll call you in a minute."

I turn away quickly, fuming and shocked and ashamed to be in this situation. The worst part is I know it's not my fault. I'm just trying to do what's right for my child whose father died. But even knowing I have no reason to feel this way doesn't make it better when someone is outright treating me like I'm garbage.

"Just ignore her."

I look up to see a woman sitting across from me. She's dressed impeccably and her makeup is spotless. She doesn't fit in this room. Maybe she's here for a job interview.

"I'm sorry?"

She flashes me a soft smile. "I said to just ignore her. She's like that every time I come in. I think she just likes to fight with people for fun."

I glance back over at the workers who are still loudly discussing my case. "And they let her get away with it?"

The woman across from me, who I guess is actually a customer like me, shrugs. "What are they gonna do? Social workers get paid terrible wages across the board to work in an office with screaming kids coming in and out all day. I'm sure the resumé pool isn't all that impressive."

A little girl I didn't notice before who is about Carson's age approaches and lays her head on the woman's lap. I smile at the gentle way she strokes the little girl's hair and I can't help but wonder about her story. She's obviously older than me by a lot, but we have a child the same age. By the way she's dressed, if I saw her on the street, I'd assume she was a business professional of some sort or maybe even a PTA mom.

"Still." I pull in a breath to calm the thoughts in my head. "It sucks to be treated like I'm trying to get away with something." I look over at my sweet boy who is still playing quietly. "His dad died in a car accident. I didn't have anything to do with that."

"Oh honey, you don't have to convince me. I'm right there with you. My ex-husband left me with three kids. My oldest is twelve and has brain damage from oxygen deprivation at birth. There is no daycare for a kiddo like him and he can't be left alone so I can't work outside my house. Especially not during holidays and summer break when there isn't even school. But people forget that part. They just assume we're out partying and popping out babies for fun, then coming in here for help cleaning up our mess."

Wow. As hard as my situation is, I can't imagine trying to provide for more than one. Even more impressive is how she can still have a decent attitude about it. "Do you ever get used to it?"

"Being treated like dirt?" I nod. "No. But you stop trying to change people's minds. My focus is on my kids, not anyone else. They all have their own crosses to bear. If I wallowed every time they tried to add to mine, I'd never get anything done."

I look at Carson again just as he glances up from the dirty toy table that probably has never been disinfected. He smiles at me like I'm his whole world, which I am. And he's mine.

If it was just me, I'd walk right out of this office and never look back. But it's not. For him, I'll suffer the humiliation. For him, I'll deal with women that have no business working in social services if they don't have an ounce of compassion in them.

"You are young and he is precious," my new friend adds. "Keep making good choices and keep putting one foot in front of the other. This is just a season in your life. I promise."

"I could say the same back to you."

She laughs. It's hearty and joyful. I hope I run into her every time I have to come in. "I wish I could believe you but it's a different animal when you have a child that's in and out of the hospital. Especially being an older mom. But it's okay. I'm strong. I'm healthy. And my prayer life has increased a million-fold since I started doing this by myself. I'll be fine. And in the meantime, I'll pretend like I've been put here to help lift people back up when someone," she glares at the lady at the front counter, "tries to bring them down."

A door opens up behind me and someone calls out, "Carson."

"That's us. Carson, come on baby."

"See? If they're taking you back it means you were right. They just had to get their thumbs out of their butts."

I pick Carson up and turn to my new friend, hoping to express the gratitude I feel. "Thank you. Truly."

"You're very welcome. Maybe we'll see each other

next time."

I give a small wave and we follow yet another person into the back offices. The appointment is quick and relatively painless. Carson would disagree since he is the one whose finger got stuck for a quick iron test. But all in all, the appointment isn't terrible. And the whole time, I think about the woman in the lobby and everything she said.

She's right. This is just a season in my life. It's a really hard season with lots of work and not lots to show for it. But I'm grateful for amazing friends, an amazing boss, and amazing strangers who can put things back into perspective.

I can choose how I respond to the boulders that drop in my way and I want to be as gracious and content as the woman I met. That means no more wallowing in the past. No more anger over Spence's betrayal or his mother's horrific treatment. No more jumping to conclusions when a nice man tries to let me down easy. All of that is over and done with. From here on out, it's a choice to be grateful for what I've been given, including a loaded WIC card to go buy some milk.

After I buckle Carson into his seat and me into mine, I take a deep breath. "Are you ready, buddy? Let's move on with our lives."

"Yeah, mama!" he yells having absolutely no idea what I'm talking about. It doesn't matter anyway. Just knowing he's with me in my fresh take on life is enough.

As I put the car in drive, my phone rings. I glance down and see it's Nicole. Quickly I connect my Bluetooth to answer.

"Hey sis. How's it going?"

"K...Ki...Kiersten?" Her voice breaks when she says my name and I can tell she's bawling. My body runs cold.

I know, I *know* what she's going to say, even though I'm praying I'm wrong. "I need your help."

"I'm on my way, baby sister. Just hold on."

Pressing on the gas, I race home. My season may be hard, but nothing is going to stop me from helping my sister through hers.

TWENTY-THREE
Paul

It's been four days since I've seen Kiersten and the guilt gets worse every minute that passes. I'm the one who drove her away. I crossed a line that never should have been crossed and consequently the exact issue I was trying to avoid happened. Kiersten was hurt in the worst way.

I'm trying not to let my emotions bleed over into the business, but I was wounded, too. I wasn't hurt in the same way she was, but it all still stings. Knowing I had one night with her, but that's all I'll ever have. Knowing I fell hard for her and can't do anything about it makes my heart feel like it's in a shredder.

"Alright, Mr. Moody." Tammy drops her tray on the counter and unloads some dirty glasses into the bucket. I ignore her nickname, too irritated to address it. "I need a house IPA, a margarita on the rocks, and an apple pie for our favorite pool shark."

I raise my eyebrows in surprise as I fill a mug with beer, careful to not make it too frothy. "Dwayne's drinking something other than water? What happened to keeping his skills sharp?"

"He said something about not having any worthy opponents tonight so he might as well booze it up instead."

I snicker. "He needs to pay more attention to the monitors up here." I gesture to the televisions hanging on the wall behind me. "The game ended a couple of hours ago. Heath already texted to let me know they're headed this way soon."

"Well shit." Tammy pauses and looks around with shifty eyes before leaning in. "Do you think I should let Dwayne know before he ends up three sheets to the wind?"

"Nah. Let people have a shot at winning their money back from him for once."

"With anyone else, I would, but I'm pretty sure this is his only form of income."

That comment should amuse me but for some reason, I find it irritating. "Maybe I need to put up a *no soliciting* sign," I grumble. "Last thing we need is a bunch of pissed off *paying* customers because he cons them out of their money."

"Well, that wasn't very kind of you. Those boys love the competition just as much as he does. And he pays his tab every night and you know it."

She's right to put me in my place. I put the glass of beer on her tray then begin pulling out the margarita mix. "You're right. I'm sorry. I don't know what's gotten into me."

"Wouldn't have anything to do with a certain dark-haired beauty that's called in sick for the last three days now would it?"

"It's been four days," I correct. "And why would my mood have anything to do with her?"

I'm a liar and we both know it.

"Since it's suddenly important to you to keep an accurate track of the calendar, maybe because you called me in five days ago so you could babysit her kid. Suddenly the next day she's taking time off." One of Tammy's eyebrows quirks up in challenge.

I accept that challenge and scoff. "Coincidence."

"I may be old, boss, but I have eyes. You wanna know my take on it?"

"No."

"Too bad." She settles against the counter and I know I may be here a while. "You and that girl have been dancing around each other for months. Finally, the one night you give in and let your feelings do the talking, suddenly she ditches work and you're in a piss poor mood for days. That's not coincidence. That's fact."

She saunters away to her customers, leaving me to chew on her words. I knew I was doing a shit job of hiding my feelings, but I didn't know I was that transparent. Or maybe I was tricking myself into believing I was keeping things to myself. Either way, I don't like that Tammy knows something happened between Kiersten and me. It's none of her business. This is the exact kind of mess I was trying to avoid. Now we're having conversations about my love life while paying customers are waiting for drinks.

"One more thing."

I finish making the margarita and roll my shoulders at the sound of her voice, trying to ward off the stress her prodding is inducing.

"Tammy," I warn as I grab the apple pie and pop the top off. "You know I don't play the boss card very often, but we have customers. Now isn't the time for this conversation."

"Our customers are completely happy right now and

like you said, we have more coming, so I better say my piece before they get here."

I want to shut her down, but the problem with Tammy is it won't work. She'll just hold onto her lecture until another time. Normally I respect that. She gives no fucks about how I might take things, so she always gives it to me straight. Tonight, though, I just want to get it over with and move on.

Sighing, I rest my hands on the counter and look her in the eyes, an unspoken request to say what she has to say so I can continue with my night.

"That girl is into you, too."

I don't respond. I was inside Kiersten just days ago. I already know how she feels. But just because Kiersten is into me doesn't mean we're supposed to do anything about it.

"I know you have this no fraternization policy you think is important or whatever. But frankly, you are missing out on something wonderful because you're worried I'm going to be jealous if you give her a little bit of nepotism? Thinking I'm going to quit if she gets a better shift than me? That girl is a hard worker and a wonderful person and any little leg up she gets, I will happily let her have. And you, my friend, are going to miss out on getting to know her better because of your misguided fear that you're going to fail me, fail her, and fail that little boy. Why do you automatically assume things are gonna go south? From what I can see, you're more likely to have a successful and satisfying relationship because you'll work for it. Failure is not an option and all that shit."

Failure is not an option.

Unexpectedly, those words hit their target.

I'm flooded with memories of my dad before he left

us. Lecturing us at the dinner table about success being the only important thing in life. In my face after getting a bad grade on a test, screaming about failure not being an option. His parting words of how we've all disappointed him by being failures as people.

I suck in a breath as I have what feels like a massive breakthrough I didn't even know was coming.

All the hesitation I've had about getting involved with Kiersten. Being hyper-focused on making sure this business is successful, no matter what the sacrifice. Stressing over how to find customers and keep them happy. Working myself to the bone to be a premier location that people want to be at, to relax, and enjoy. Shoving aside relationships to keep drama out of my business and my life.

Terrified I'm going to fail.

Failure is not an option.

I hear the words in my mind again, only this time I'm not the one saying them. My father is.

It was him. It was always him in the back of my mind that has created a fear of failure. And for what? To please a man I haven't seen in decades? Who died with not one penny to his own name because he was such a great example of practicing what he preached?

I feel like I've been hit in the head by a sledgehammer as everything shifts inside me. I don't have to please him. I can fail if I want and he'll never even know. Wouldn't matter if he did anyway. It's not his life. It's mine. If I want to take a chance on a woman who makes me happy and keeps me smiling, I can. And if it doesn't work out, at least I can say I tried.

I must have a stunned look on my face because Tammy smiles like the cat that ate the canary.

"Realizing I'm right, aren't you? Does that mean

you're going to do something about it?"

It takes a few seconds before my head stops spinning and I can get my words in order to respond. I finally nod sheepishly knowing the first thing I need to do is apologize to the woman I hurt. "I think I need to, don't you?"

She bangs one hand on the counter. "Thank goodness you finally figured it out. I was getting tired of wading through the sexual tension every night."

"Let's not get ahead of ourselves. I still have some amends to make and it's up to her if she forgives me."

"At least that snowball is finally moving in the right direction, though." Tammy grabs the tray and turns to walk away then thinks better of it. "And another thing!" she yells.

What could she possibly be talking about now?

"We need more help around here. If we're going to have all these hunky guys drinking every night, you need to start looking to hire a couple of people. At this point, there is no way this place is going to fail, even if you try to sabotage it. Give this old woman a break."

She's making a lot of sense tonight about a lot of things. Not for the first time, I'm, grateful she stayed when I took over.

"Noted. I'll post some want adds to find a new wait-ress."

"And a new bartender. Plan to succeed, boss. We're gonna need both."

The front door opens and the humidity hits me like a freight train. So does the sound of a dozen or so profes-sional football players celebrating a win. It's go time as the team starts to trickle in. Frankie goes straight to Tammy for a kiss on the cheek, which makes her blush and giggle, then goes to sit at his favorite booth.

Tammy and I hustle for a solid hour plus as drinks are ordered and served. This is what I love—when we're busy and customers are happy, significant others joining in to give their congratulations on a well-deserved win.

The only one seemingly not happy is Dwayne, who realizes he made a bad choice on drinking tonight. I can't help but chuckle at his bad luck. Tammy's right about him. He's a staple in this bar and if this is where he's happy and comfortable, it doesn't really matter what anyone else thinks. I appreciate Tammy reminding me of that, even if it makes me feel like a dick sometimes.

Things finally start to settle into a steady but manageable pace when Heath and Lauren walk in. Heath gestures hello to me and heads for his team. Lauren, on the other hand, walks up to the bar. I have a feeling we're about to have a heart to heart.

"Before you start, are you here to order, or are you going to berate me, too? Because Tammy already did."

"I like Tammy more and more," Lauren says under her breath as she slides on the stool. "I could rip you a new one but I've only heard bits and pieces of your night together, which incidentally it's about damn time. But Kiersten has bigger fish to fry right now so I'll save it until a later date. Can I get whatever ale you have on tap?"

"Sure. And what do you mean she has bigger fish to fry? Is something else going on? I thought she was just trying to get away from me."

"Don't give yourself so much credit. Kiersten has been thoroughly dicked over in ways you can't even imagine. Your little fickle act doesn't mean all that much."

I wince at the harshness of her words. I don't like being lumped into the category of "men who have screwed Kiersten over." I also don't like knowing there is a category at all.

"It's not me being fickle."

She gives me a disbelieving look but says nothing.

"It's not about not being sure of my feelings. It's… according to Tammy, well, according to me too, it's fear."

Lauren takes a drink, showing no reaction to what felt like a huge revelation to me. "Of what?"

"Failing her."

"Seems to me you already did."

"I know. And I've spent a part of tonight thinking about how to fix it. How to get over myself, I guess," I say with a deep sigh. "I don't want to yank her around."

"She won't let you anyway. You may have some deep fear of commitment or whatever, but she's been burned in the hardest way. And one thing I know of Kiersten is she might give you a second chance. Might. But there won't be a third. You better be damn sure you don't squander it."

"I won't."

"See that you don't." Lauren slides off the stool, and I assume this conversation is over. But I need to know one more thing before she gets back to her friends.

"Hey, Lauren."

She looks me in the eye, waiting for whatever I have to say.

"Is she okay? Is Carson? I should have checked on them. I was… I thought I was giving her space." I could kick myself for assuming Kiersten's disappearance was about me.

Lauren's eyes soften as she takes in my very genuine concern. "They're fine. It's not my story to tell, but I will say you need to talk to her. I have a feeling you are the only one who can provide the kind of support she needs right now."

I nod as ideas begin running through my brain on how I can be there for Kiersten. I don't know what exactly is going on, but I need to make this right. And I won't make this same mistake again.

TWENTY-FOUR

Kiersten

My back aches from carrying boxes and my whole body is still sore from driving. I'm mentally and physically exhausted, and yet, I'm still going. I don't have a choice right now. I can't stop. I *won't* stop.

Bleary-eyed, I settle on instant oatmeal for breakfast this morning. It's not Carson's favorite, but anything that only requires one hand for eating is easier for Nicole. Right now, that's my priority.

"Mama!" Carson yells despite my near-constant shushing. "Mama, I hungee!"

I give him my best stern look, but he doesn't tear his eyes from the television, instead, continuing his demands.

"Mama!"

Huffing, I walk his plastic bowl to the small table before approaching him. "Carson, your food is on the table. Now stop yelling. NicNic is sleeping."

"No, she's not."

My sister comes shuffling out of the bedroom, careful not to move too quickly. It takes everything in me not to react to her appearance, knowing it only makes things harder when I do. But that doesn't mean my heart doesn't feel like it stalls whenever I take her in.

When I first met her at the hospital, her hair was matted and she had blood all over her face mixed in with mascara that at some point had been dripping down her cheeks before it dried. I don't know how long that little shit Jeremy spent beating her, but it was enough to leave her with a black eye, a broken nose, a fractured wrist, and bruises covering most of her body. And still, as hard as I tried, as hard as the social worker tried, Nicole won't press charges.

The only good news is the statute of limitations gives her two years to change her mind. Pictures of her injuries were taken, a police report was filed, and I have all the officer's information. When my sister is ready, I'll be right here helping her through the legal process.

The other good news is the college allowed her to withdraw, effective immediately, with no penalty to her transcript. I'm almost positive it's because the dean saw her face, so he pulled some strings. Whether it was out of the kindness of his heart or because he's afraid they'll end up on the news due to the beating happening on campus, I'm not sure. Either way, it gives Nicole the ability to start college over when she's ready.

For now, the only thing I know for certain is she's moved in with me, disconnected her phone, and shut down all her social media. It's still not locking that asshole up, but I have to give her credit for at least getting away from him. One step at a time.

Gingerly, she sits down at the table just in time for me to place her oatmeal in front of her.

"How are you feeling this morning?"

"Sore," she says as she picks up her spoon and slowly

begins to eat.

"Do you need a painkiller?"

She nods. "Yeah, my wrist is really aching this morning."

Anger surges through me when she mentions the pain she's in. It's a good thing Jeremy never showed his face at the hospital. Jail time is nothing compared to the things I want to do to him for hurting my baby sister.

We get settled at the table, quietly eating our food. Well, most of us are quiet. Carson is wiggling in his seat as always and humming a song he probably made up. Just as he goes to take a big bite, he stops and looks at Nicole.

"Why you hurt, NicNic?"

My heart squeezes with hurt as I watch his wide, innocent eyes take in her appearance. I wonder what conclusions his little mind is coming to and if this is the first of many times he will learn that life is sometimes cruel. I hate that. I hate that at just three years old he's already seeing the reality of how ugly people can be to each other.

Nicole puts down her spoon and turns all her attention on him. "There was a very bad man who hurt me. But I'm okay, buddy."

"A bad man?"

"Yes. But he's veeeery far away. And he can't hurt me anymore. The police took him and I'm safe now."

That's not totally accurate, but I appreciate her trying to give him truthful information without making him scared.

"Chase took bad man?"

I smile at how his little brain immediately thinks of his favorite Paw Patrol character as the policeman who saved the day. Nicole smiles, too and I'm glad to see she can find some amusement in all this.

"Yep. Chase helped me and now everything is okay."

Carson thinks hard for a few seconds before nodding once and shoving more oatmeal in his mouth.

I smirk and turn to my sister. "Paw Patrol for the win."

She giggles and I love hearing that sound. To me, it means she's on the road to healing. Physically and mentally.

"Um… has mom called?" My sister looks up at me, her eyes practically begging me to tell her what she wants to hear. But I can't be honest and make her feel better at the same time.

I shake my head. "I'm sorry."

Tears fill her eyes but she quickly blinks them away. "Well, I guess that's our answer, isn't it?"

I grab her hand and squeeze, understanding how hard it is when our mother makes her rejection clear. In my case, however, I got Carson out of the deal. Nicole has just been left on her own with nothing to cling to.

As it turns out, I was the second phone call Nicole made after arriving at the hospital. The first was to our mother who hurried to the ER like any good mother would. When she got there, however, and heard Nicole's claims, her immediate response was to tell my honest-to-the-bone sister to stop making up stories that could ruin lives.

I wasn't there when it happened but heard all about it from my sister when I tried to call mom to keep her updated. To say I was shocked would be an understatement. Blaming me for getting pregnant is one thing. Blaming Nicole for getting beat up by her boyfriend is a whole different level of low, even for our mother.

She hasn't tried to make contact since she was escorted out of the room by the caseworker who was less than thrilled about mom's lack of support.

Now, we're on our own. And as glad as I am that I can

be here to support Nicole, I admit to feeling some nerves about having another mouth to feed. I could pull Carson out of daycare, but Heath is still the one fronting that bill so it won't make any difference. Plus, Nicole is in no physical shape to care for a toddler. It'll all work out somehow, I just don't have any idea how at this point.

A knock at the door has us shaking off the moment, grateful for a distraction. I leave the two of them to finish their breakfast and go to answer the door. Looking through the peephole, I'm surprised by who I see on the other side.

Pulling the door open, my surprise bleeds through. "Paul?"

"Hi." His voice is quiet and if I'm hearing it correctly, tinged with a bit of humility.

"What are you doing here?"

"I talked to Lauren last night."

"Ah." I should have guessed she would end up at the bar at some point and she's never been one to hold her tongue.

"I don't know what's going on, but I know you have bigger issues right now than me and my fear of failure."

That is not what I expected him to say. Not only did he just admit the fight we had stems from something deeper than just a misunderstanding, but he's pushing it aside until the more important issues can be fixed. I hate that it makes me want to forgive him, but there it is. And yet, he's not done.

"I brought some supplies." He holds up some canvas grocery sacks I hadn't noticed until now. "I know you can take care of yourself, but I hope it takes some of the pressure off while you sort out, well, whatever."

Stunned by his thoughtfulness, although I probably shouldn't be surprised since he tends to be a thoughtful guy, I wave him in. He continues to ramble on about what he brought.

"I brought mostly pantry stuff that wouldn't go bad." He places the bags on the couch and begins riffling through them. "Um, I found some little graham cracker bites that are shaped like Paw Patrol characters. I figured Carson would get a kick out of that. And since he likes puzzles, I picked up a new one so he would have something to do if you need him to be entertained while you sort out stuff. Oh, this needs to go in the fridge. It's a little Paw Patrol snack pack with cheese and grapes and stuff in it."

I take it from him when he hands it to me, moved by how sweet it was for him to focus more on Carson being taken care of than me. It's like he knows if my child is okay, I will be, too.

"Thank you," I say quietly. "He's going to love all of it."

Shoving his hands in his front pockets, Paul opens his mouth to say something, but Carson takes that exact moment to race into the room and head straight for our guest.

"Paw! Paw!" he yells and wraps his arms around Paul's legs for a hug. Without hesitation, Paul picks him up and wraps his arms tightly around Carson's little body.

"Hey, bud. How are you? Are you being good for mommy?"

Carson pulls away and begins babbling like only he can. "NicNic here and Chase take bad man away."

Paul looks at me with confusion. "Chase what? Was that an episode of…"

I don't have to look behind me to know my sister just came into the room. It's clear by the look on Paul's face he's putting everything together—my sudden disappearance, Lauren's refusal to share information, why our fight is the least of my concerns.

To his credit, he very quickly schools his features and makes no move to touch her. It's like he's consciously making sure he doesn't scare her with sudden movements and noises.

"I assume you're who this little guy calls NicNic." Paul presses his fingers into Carson's tummy, making him squeal with delight, and again I appreciate that he's pretending to be nonchalant, even though I can see the rage in his eyes.

My sister clears her throat before speaking. She's been doing that a lot. I assume her throat must be hurting if Jeremy squeezed her neck at all, but I haven't been brave enough to ask yet.

"That's me. Most people just call me Nicole, though."

"Well, it's nice to meet you, Nicole. Will you be staying with Kiersten for a while?"

The question seems innocent, but I can read between the lines. He wants to make sure she's out of a bad situation and safe now.

"For as long as she'll let me."

We all stand there awkwardly, her words sinking in. There's not really a response when someone admits their life is in complete limbo and there are no plans for the future. But my sister knows me well, so she jumps in.

"Why don't Carson and I color for a little bit and you guys can talk in the kitchen?"

"Color!" Carson yells and wiggles his way out of Paul's arms and onto the floor. He runs off leaving Paul free to grab the bags and follow me into the kitchen.

"You really didn't have to do this," I say as we begin unloading everything he brought.

"Honestly, I wasn't sure how to help since I didn't

know what was wrong. Now I'm glad I brought food." He tilts his head toward the living room. "I take it your swift departure was about Nicole?"

I nod sadly. "She called me from the hospital the morning after… well, you know what morning I'm talking about."

"I'm sorry. I can't imagine what kind of a shock it must have been."

"I think at first I just went on autopilot. But when I saw her…" I bite my bottom lip. I don't want to cry again. She's just in the other room and I won't let her see me get teary. I can't. My job is to be her strength. I take a few moments and when I feel stronger, I finish my sentence. "She's cleaned up now so it doesn't look as bad as it did. But yes, I have images in my brain I will never forget."

"What can I do?"

"Honestly, I don't know. I'm really glad tips are good right now. It'll make it easier to feed everyone. Mostly, I think she needs time. She startles easily and she's embarrassed. I kind of want to bring her with me to work for a while so she's not here alone and afraid, but I don't know if just being around the guys will scare her."

"Maybe if Heath talks to them and makes sure everyone leaves her alone, she'll actually feel more protected with them around."

I nod because it's definitely something to think about. I know I'd feel more secure with her at the bar. Logically, it's unlikely Jeremy will drive all the way out here to find her, but you just never know with guys like him.

"Anyway, if she wants to come with you, I'm okay with that. We can let her hang out in the office or she can even stay at my apartment if she wants."

"I don't think she'll be comfortable being alone with

you at your place."

"I won't be back there much. Tammy is hounding me to hire some new people. I need to get on that. Create ads and all that crap again."

"Tammy's not wrong. I know it's not official until you hit the six-month mark in the black or whatever, but I think it's a safe bet to call yourself a successful business owner at this point. It can only get busier from here."

He chuckles. "You aren't the first person to tell me that over the last couple of days."

"Why don't you believe us?"

Paul's eyes seem to get sad at my question. I may have struck a nerve.

"My dad was a real son of a bitch. Rode us kids hard on everything. *Don't quit until it's perfect. Failure is not an option.* He had like this military mindset when it came to raising kids."

Paul looks at the floor, refusing to make eye contact with me. Whether it's from embarrassment or because he's visualizing memories, I'm not sure. The only thing I know is I'm seeing a side of Paul I'm certain he doesn't show most people.

"He constantly drilled into our heads that we were nothing unless we were successful, that the worst thing we could ever do is fail. The irony of it is he didn't stick around long enough to teach us how to succeed. He left us with no tools for achievement, only a psyche that always struggles with the fear of mistakes."

Paul looks up, lips quirking up on one side like he's trying to smile but can't quite get there. "I like you so much, Kiersten. More than like. I've been falling for you since, hell I don't even know how long it's been. I'm also terrified I'll fuck it all up and leave you and Carson as damaged as he left me."

I'm speechless. Completely at a loss for words at the bomb he just dropped. Images flood my brain of a future with Paul. Thoughts of what could be. I allow myself just a small moment to enjoy it before pulling myself back to reality. Because it doesn't matter how Paul feels. What matters is how he acts. And that's not something I can trust yet.

"I really loved Spence." Paul winces at the name, which doesn't go unnoticed or unappreciated by me, as much as I hate to admit it. "I had my eyes wide open during that relationship and as it turns out, it didn't matter. The wool was still pulled over them. I'm not sure if we were a game to him or what, but I am fully convinced if he hadn't died, he would have yanked me and Carson around until I accidentally found out about his real life."

"He was a dick."

"He was probably a clinical narcissist," I clarify. "But that's beside the point. What Spence taught me is that pretty words are really nice to hear, but without action to back it up, there's no substance."

"I know," Paul says quietly. "That's why I brought food. I wanted to show you I'm not just talk. I'm action."

"And it was a really nice action. But I can't ignore the red flags all over the place, Paul. Red flags you planted."

He digs his hands into his pockets, a move I've discovered he does when he's nervous. "You're right."

"I know. So, you can see why I'm hesitant. I know all of this is your way of apologizing, which I fully accept. But that doesn't mean I'm ready to take the next step with you."

He holds my gaze but I can see the determination in his eyes.

"I understand. And I accept that. I broke your trust with

my flippant words and fickle behavior. But Kiersten," he takes a step toward me, close enough I have to lift my head to maintain eye contact. "I will win your trust back. I don't like knowing my flippant use of words made you take a step back. I've missed you the last few days and I don't ever want to feel like this again."

"I've missed you too." I fight to keep my arms from wrapping around his neck, when all I want to do is let him hold me. "But I can't."

He tucks a stray hair behind my ear, the brush of his finger making me shiver. "I know. And I respect that. I just wanted you to know where my brain is at."

He backs away slowly, never taking his locked gaze off me before he turns on his heel and walks out my front door, leaving me to my swirling thoughts.

TWENTY-FIVE
Paul

The last few days have been nothing short of a nightmare.

They've also been a tremendous relief.

It's a dichotomy I'm still trying to wrap my brain around, but I try to remind myself of the important things.

The most important being Kiersten is back. You wouldn't know by talking to her that she and I had a falling out of sorts. Or at least, no one else would. I can still see the reservation on her face when we interact. It's clear she doesn't trust me, which I deserve. I hurt her with my words. It takes time for the sting to go away. But she's still fun and engaging with the customers and I like that. She still takes time to cut a rug with Dwayne on the dance floor. The only time her demeanor is different is when she talks to her sister. I'm not sure if Kiersten's energy tones down because she doesn't want to overwhelm Nicole or because she doesn't want to overwhelm herself, but the change is definitely there.

Nicole has been hanging out a lot, which is fine by me.

At first, she stayed in the office, but after a couple of days, I guess she got bored and ventured out. Now she spends most of her time sitting on the last stool next to the bar—the seat that allows her to have her back to the wall and her side next to the counter. All she does is people watch. Granted, there is all kinds of action when you have some of the most testosterone-filled, competitive men in the world hanging out in your bar. She might actually be onto something. I bet she sees some interesting things none of their agents would like getting out.

On the flip side, I've been dealing with one hell of a shit show putting together ads and fielding calls from prospective employees. I don't know how many of these people have actually worked in a bar before, but they don't seem to understand you don't call after ten at night and try to get the boss on the line. Drinks are flowing and people are drunk by then. Unless you're an Uber trying to find your customer, I don't have time to stop and chat.

Disgruntled from sorting through applications again and coming up absolutely empty, I push away from my desk and make my way to the front. I could use some caffeine and a change of scenery.

I'm greeted by hoots and hollers, but they aren't for me.

"What's going on over there?" I ask Nicole as I pass by. The more time she spends here, the more comfortable she's become with me. She's a nice girl. Quiet, understandably. But friendly enough. And she doesn't mince words on her opinions about what goes on in here sometimes. Kind of like Tammy, except gentler. I like that.

"From what I've gathered, some new guy is getting his rear handed to him at pool."

"Is Dwayne involved?" I purse my lips. I'd bet money

I already know the answer to this question.

"Of course."

I shake my head indignantly. "That man has got to stop scamming all my customers."

"It wasn't his fault this time. I think the new guy is a rookie so his teammates are hazing him or something."

I grunt. "I guess I'll let it go. But that man and I are gonna have a chat one of these days."

"Leave him be, boss." Tammy joins our conversation as she approaches. "That rookie deserves to have his ass handed to him. He's been talking smack all night. I think the rest of his team finally got tired of it. They're enjoying watching Dwayne take him for his signing bonus."

A shot of adrenaline runs through me and my eyes widen. "Please tell me there's not that much money on the line."

Tammy waves me off like I'm being ridiculous. "I'm sure it's not that much."

That does not make me feel any better.

"Let's just say Dwayne is gonna be able to make rent this month with no problem."

I hang my head, shaking it back and forth. "We're gonna get shut down. I just know it. The gaming commission is gonna show up and accuse me of illegal gambling."

Kiersten joins the conversation, placing freshly made drinks on Tammy's tray. I love seeing things run like a well-oiled machine.

"Stop being a Debbie Downer," she chides as she grabs beer mugs and begins filling them. "They're just having a good time. That's what we want, right?"

I sigh in resignation. She's right. They're all right. This is what we've been working for and now I'm focusing on the wrong things. I guess I have more work to do on my insecurities than I realized.

"Fine. Let them have their fun. I'll back off."

"Can I get you something, Paul?" Kiersten asks as she tops off the glasses. "You look like you could use a shot of caffeine."

"We don't have any coffee, do we? The fresh stuff. Not yesterday's batch warmed up."

"I actually brewed some a little bit ago. Customer request."

"Perfect." I climb under the counter to grab it myself.

"How's the bartender search going anyway?"

I puff out an exasperated breath. Maybe this coffee will take the edge off. "It shouldn't be this hard to find a waitress. Hey, Nicole," I call over my shoulder. "You wanna be a waitress? I hear the boss is amazing to work for."

She shakes her head vigorously, eyes wide with fright. I can understand that. She sits with her back against the wall every night. I guess she's not ready to walk around amongst everyone yet.

"I've seen the responses online. Lots of people seem interested. Are you sure you're not being too picky?"

"Yes. No. I don't have any idea. Ideally, I'd like someone with experience, but that's not what's making me gun shy."

I turn to lean against the counter and sip my drink. It hits the spot.

"What's the problem?"

"See those guys out there?" We both watch the scene at the pool table as it unfolds. There are smiles and laughter. People are clapping each other on the back and even Dwayne fits right in. "They're comfortable letting their hair down and just having a good time. I don't want to ruin that. Anyone who works here needs to be discreet.

You were an easy hire because you already know these guys. This is your circle so you get it. Not everyone will. I don't want the wrong person working here who blows the lid off everything."

"I see. It's less about finding someone who can do the job and more about finding someone you can trust."

"Exactly. How in the world am I supposed to find that from a few online applications?"

Kiersten wipes her hands on a towel and flings it over her shoulder. "That's a tough one. I might have an idea though."

"I'm open to anything at this point."

"Jaxon's brother is going to school here now and I'm pretty sure he mentioned that he's looking for a job."

I furrow my brow. That doesn't sound right for some reason. "Isn't his brother in high school or something?"

"His other brother."

Again, what am I missing? "Wait, Jaxon has another brother?"

"I think Kade is his birth dad's son or something? I don't remember how all that works. I just know he's a freshman at Southeast and he's paying all his own expenses. I accidentally overheard the conversation so that's all I know. But with it being Jaxon's brother…"

"He's got some experience with the world of professional football," I finish for her, my brain already thinking through what kind of a fit he could be.

"That would be my guess. At the very least, Jaxon might be able to help you explain why discretion is important while working here."

"That's a really good idea, Kiersten. Thank you." I take another drink, not ready to go back to the office, which feels more like a cave right now. Instead, I take a few minutes to watch Kiersten work. She's mesmerizing to me. The graceful way she moves. The beautiful way she smiles at people. The way that smile never quite leaves her plump lips, even when she's not speaking with anyone.

"I miss you."

I don't mean to say the words out loud, but they've left my lips before I can stop them. I don't regret it, but I'm not sure from the look Kiersten gives me if they're welcome.

"I miss you, too," she finally says quietly. "But that doesn't mean I've changed my mind."

"I know. I guess I just want you to know my feelings haven't changed."

"Hey, Kiersten," Tammy yells interrupting the moment. "I got a big order for ya."

The woman I love turns away from me and begins the task of pulling together buckets of ice, bottles of beer, and the occasional mixed beverage. Tammy's not kidding it's a big order. Seems like everyone in this place got thirsty at the same time.

"The game is over and they're celebrating Dwayne's victory," Tammy exclaims with delight. I guess she was more invested in the game than I realized.

I jump in and help them gather everything, most of which doesn't even fit on Tammy's tray. This is going to take several trips.

"Do you mind taking these over to the booth?" Tammy asks Kiersten, gesturing over her shoulder to Frankie's favorite spot. Frankie isn't here tonight, but he's not the only one who seems to like that high-back booth.

"Sure thing. Can you cover me back here?" Kiersten asks me but doesn't wait for an answer before she takes off to make the delivery. Like I said, some things work like clockwork around here.

"While she's out of earshot and I have the chance, I need you to listen to me and listen good." The forcefulness of Tammy's words make me take pause. "I don't know what you did to make things worse, but I'm tired of you two pining over each other from a distance. It's time for you to make a big gesture."

Fancy words coming from someone who's feelings aren't on the line. "Some romance novel shit is not going to win her over. I just need to keep proving I'm trustworthy. Slow and steady and all that."

"That's hogwash and you know it." Tammy points her finger at me and I'm taken slightly aback at her aggressiveness. "Every woman wants a grand gesture, especially if you spend most of your time being private."

I open my mouth to argue but she cuts me off before I can say a word.

"No. You listen to me. Putting yourself on the line in private is one thing, but there's no accountability in that. Putting yourself on the line in public? That means a whole lot of people will be pissed off at you if you don't follow through. See the difference?"

Oddly, I do. I hadn't thought of it that way. I look over at Nicole for confirmation.

She nods in agreement. "Everything Spence did was private. His parents are still trying to keep his sins private. No one has ever put themselves out there for her publicly."

And now I feel like an idiot. Of course, she feels like I'm not trustworthy. My intentions might be different, but I'm treating our relationship the exact same way Spence did. Like it's something that doesn't need to be discussed publicly. To me, it's because I don't want to screw it up. I want to keep it to myself so no outside influences cause problems. But to her, it's reminiscent of the worst blow she's ever been dealt.

I need to fix this, I'm just not sure how.

My eyes search the room quickly, looking for her. I should have known I'd find her on the dance floor, helping celebrate with Dwayne. That man is holding one of her hands while he shows off some fancy footwork. Kiersten's face is radiating joy as she keeps up with whatever steps he throws at her.

I can't help when my lips quirk up. She does that to me. Even just watching her makes me feel happy.

Tammy snickers next to me. "Nothing that girl loves more than taking a spin around the dance floor."

And that's when an idea begins to form. If she needs a grand gesture, I think I have the perfect one.

TWENTY-SIX
Kiersten

"Bye, buddy. Have fun at school."

Carson runs into his classroom without looking back.

"Harumph," I grumble under my breath. "I see how it is."

Nicole laughs lightly next to me. "At least he likes his daycare. Not everyone can say that." She doesn't have to gesture behind her for me to know who she's talking about. It's pretty clear by how long the shrieking has been going on in the hallway that one of the two-year-olds still has his mother in a chokehold while his teacher tries to untangle his arms.

"Sometimes I wish Carson loved me like that."

"It'll only make things weird when he's my age."

She's got a point. And she's right, it is good that he enjoys school because he's going to be spending more time here today. Paul called me in to work early. Something about not having time for inventory at night anymore so we need to do it during the day. The words themselves made sense, but it was the tone he used that made me question his truthfulness.

Or maybe it's just me still struggling with the stalemate that we've found ourselves in.

I've been stuck in my head ever since our fall out and all the thinking time has led me to a realization. I'm in love with Paul. Bone deep, soul defying love. And while people think love heals all wounds, it doesn't. It doesn't even come close. And that's where I'm stuck. I'm not fully healed from the scars that cover my soul and not even loving Paul can change that.

"Thanks for letting me drop him early," I say with a wave to the director as we walk past her office on our way out.

"No problem. Heath pays for full-time care in case you need it so it's yours to use."

My only response is a shake of my head. Of course, he pays for full-time daycare. That's something only Heath would feel is a good investment—daycare *just in case* it's needed. I make a mental note to thank him once again. At this point, it's the only thing I can do. There's no way I'll ever be able to repay him for everything.

Nicole and I climb into my car and head to Frui Vita several hours ahead of my normal schedule. Paul has assured me he'll let me go home early as well, but I have my doubts. Inventory alone can go on for hours. And if I'm still there when the first batch of patrons come in, there's no way I'll be out of there before closing time. Not with only three of us working. I really hope he followed up with Jaxon's brother. I have no idea if he'll be a good fit, but at this point, he seems like our best bet.

I pull into the gravel lot and park in my normal space in the middle. It's not at the front but has the best lighting for leaving in the middle of the night. It's also right next to a giant black truck which is odd.

"Why are there a bunch of cars here? How many people did he call in to help?"

Nicole shrugs but doesn't answer, likely as confused as I am. Once again, I question how truthful Paul was being when we talked about my shift change today. Not that it's a bad thing to have more help. I just don't understand what's going on.

My sister doesn't seem to be having the same existential crisis I'm suffering from. She's halfway through the parking lot before I'm out of the car, which is yet another odd thing. Normally she's stuck by my side like glue. *What is with everyone today? Am I overthinking literally everything?*

Shaking off my random thoughts, I hustle through the door only to find well over a dozen people inside. They're all women, many with familiar faces, and they're all congregating on the dance floor, smiling and laughing as if they're anticipating the start of something. But what?

I approach the bar my boss is standing behind as he dries some freshly cleaned glasses.

"How many people did you recruit for inventory and why are we using customers to help?"

"I have a confession." He chuckles lightly and puts the glass away, tossing the towel over his shoulder. "I didn't call you in for inventory."

"I kinda got that. Then why am I here?"

Paul taps his fingers on the bar for a split second and then tosses the towel on the counter to make his way underneath. "Follow me."

Intrigued by what was clearly a set up on his part, I do as he instructs. I glance at my sister when we pass by but something in her expression has me looking twice. My jaw drops as it dawns on me.

"You helped set me up, didn't you?"

She shrugs again, a sweet and innocent look on her face but she's not fooling me. I've seen it before. She used to give it to me on Christmas and birthday mornings when she pulled off an unexpectedly thoughtful gift. Now I'm really curious.

"Ladies," Paul claps his hands together. "Thank you for waiting an extra few minutes before we begin. You guys know Kiersten."

He gestures to me and they all cheer. I respond with an awkward wave. I'm not one who normally minds being put on the spot, I'm pretty quick-witted, but the more they look at me with the expectation of something I'm in the dark about, the more concerned I become.

"She doesn't know why she's here," Paul admits to the crowd. "Some of you are privy to why. Others of you are just now finding out this information, but let me assure you, from what I know, Kiersten is the best and she will rise to the challenge. Your money will be well spent, I promise."

"It better be," Lauren shouts making the other women laugh, but I see it on her face. Whatever is happening, she's in on it too. And she has full confidence I will rise to this challenge.

Paul turns to me and takes a deep breath, nerves written all over his face. My heart responds by beating faster. For whatever reason, this moment feels huge. Life-altering huge. Or again, maybe I'm reading into things that aren't there. Either way, I find myself holding my breath.

"I made a huge mistake keeping my feelings for you private."

I blink multiple times. Of all the things I expected him to say, which wasn't many considering I have no idea what's happening, that wasn't it.

"It wasn't because I was embarrassed or ashamed or because I was keeping you my dirty little secret. It just felt like something really important and delicate and I didn't want anyone getting in the middle of it and screwing it up."

A few of the women react with sounds of awe and I'm sure more than one of them clutches their chest. But I'm focusing on Paul as he takes a step forward and grabs my hands, like he's anchoring himself to me as he bares his soul.

"I'm so in love with you it makes me stupid. But it also makes me scared. I'm so afraid I'm going to fail you and Carson that I tried to push you away to protect you both. I don't want to do that anymore, Kiersten. That's why I'm saying it in front of all these ladies here. Because I know if I screw up, if I get even close to failing you, these ladies right here will have something to say about it."

"Damn straight!"

I'm not sure who calls out, but it makes everyone laugh, including me. It's a welcome feeling and narrows my eyes just enough to squeeze out the tears I've been try-ing to hold back.

"I know it's going to take some time for you to trust me again, but I'm going to woo you, Kiersten Willoughby. And I'm going to do it publicly so there's never any doubt in your mind that you're worth all the embarrassment and humiliation the men these ladies are attached to will no doubt give me every night."

I have no response, completely speechless. Instead, I wipe the tears off my cheeks and sniff, overcome with the emotion he makes me feel. For the first time, I understand the depth of his feelings for me and I'm not afraid.

"I love you, too. So much. And I look forward to being wooed by you."

I don't think I've ever seen a bigger smile on Paul's face than right now.

"Really?"

"Really. Now kiss me and make it official."

He doesn't hesitate, just grabs my hips and steps into my space, kissing me like his life depends on it. He nips and sucks on my bottom lip and I'm fully invested in the feel of his lips on mine, I barely hear the hoots and hollers surrounding us. After a few minutes, or hours, or seconds because *what is time?*, he takes a step back, but keeps hold of my hand.

"Before we embarrass ourselves any further," he says making all of us chuckle again. "I need to introduce you to your first dance class."

Everything comes to a screeching halt. "My what?"

"I know how much you loved teaching dance classes before you started working here. And I know you've always wanted to open your own studio."

I know Lauren shared that information. I glare at her, and she responds by shrugging like she thinks my feelings are irrelevant.

"I don't really have the money to front a whole new business so with the help of a few friends," he makes a point of looking directly at Lauren and Nicole individually, confirming my suspicions. "We decided this might be a good place to start."

"I… I don't understand." I really am lost. The words all make sense but this is such a huge endeavor, I can't wrap my brain around it.

He smiles, seeming to understand how hard it is for me to comprehend. "All these ladies want to learn how to dance. They've seen you taking a break on the dance floor at night and know you're the perfect person to teach them."

My head whips over to look at the crowd of women again. "Really?" I'm answered with a chorus of nods and smiles.

"They've each paid thirty bucks for an hour and a half lesson today. And all that money is yours to pocket. No fees or anything since I'm already here and getting ready to open. I even got you some business cards." He licks his lips and pulls something out of his back pocket. "I took a guess on the logo. We can change it, of course. But it has the office number on it so you can bring in more customers."

He hands me the small card that says "Willoughby Dance" in large script letters with a picture of a willow tree covering the side. It's beautiful and classy and exactly what I would have chosen if I was creative enough to think of it.

"I wasn't sure about the willow tree, but it reminded me of the way you move on the dance floor, all graceful. Plus, it seemed like a fun play on words with your last name. If you hate them, we can throw them out and start over from scratch."

A blush covers his face as he shares his thought process, obviously not used to sharing so much about his feelings in public. I'm still having a hard time following though.

"Hold on. Let me make sure I understand. Everyone is here for me to teach them how to dance and I'm getting paid for it?"

He nods, his lips quirking up on the side. "I wasn't really sure how much to charge. I just guessed this first time. Should I have charged more? I can pay the difference if I got it wrong," he adds quickly.

"No. No that's about right. I just… why?"

A slight shrug ripples through his shoulders. "Because it matters to you."

All the breath leaves my lungs. This sweet man coordinated the beginning of a new venture for me in my chosen industry. He believes in me enough that he's allowing me to use his own business to front mine.

Turning to the ladies who are waiting patiently, I ask, "Can you guys give me just one second?" and then I drag Paul off to the side, out of earshot.

"I'm sorry if I overstepped," he begins before I have time to say a word. "Lauren and Nicole assured me you would love it. I never thought—"

I cut him off by pressing my lips to his, trying to convey how grateful I am. It takes a moment for him to realize what's happening and then he's kissing me back. But I'm determined to talk this through. We haven't done enough of that lately.

Allowing myself to fall back down on my heels, I keep my arms around his neck. "I love you. I've loved you for a long time. I was just too scared to let you in. I'd like to say things would be different if I didn't have Carson, but I'm not sure. I think I'm a little gun-shy still."

"Justifiably."

"No. No I don't think so. The part of this whole story that I seem to have forgotten is that Spence was the life of the party. Always. He loved attention. He loved walking into a room and being greeted with slaps on the back and being handed a beer."

"Sounds like a douchebag," Paul says dryly.

"It depends on whose opinion you're getting," I say with a laugh. "But the key should have been how he loved attention but kept me secret. Do you know he told me he didn't have any social media? That's why he never posted any pictures of us."

Paul's brows furrow. "Is that weird? I don't have social media."

"It's not weird for you, because you're a private person by nature. It was weird for him because he was a social butterfly. I found out later he did have social media. But if he'd shared that little tidbit with me, I would have figured out his game long before I did."

Paul closes his eyes and takes a deep breath. I know he's trying to calm himself down from thinking about all the ways Spence treated me like trash.

"Hey." I nudge him. "My point isn't to make you angry about Spence's behavior. My point is I screwed up. I should have recognized you wanting to keep our relationship quiet was because you treasured it, not because you were playing me. Instead, I jumped to conclusions. I'm sorry for that."

Paul rests his forehead against mine and breathes me in. "Say it again."

"What?"

"That you love me. Say it again."

The smile comes before the words do. "I love you. So much. And I'm excited to see where we go from here."

The sigh that comes from him is one of true contentment. I know, because I feel the exact same way. But we can't stay like this forever.

"Now, if you'll excuse me, I have paying clients who came for some dance lessons."

He kisses me on the tip of my nose. "Knock 'em dead."

Turning back towards the group I fly by the seat of my pants and get this class started.

"Okay ladies, since I didn't have a lot of time to plan, what do you say we work on some line dances today?"

The response I get is overwhelmingly pleased and I can't help how big the smile on my face is. I love dance. I love teaching dance. And I love the man that gave it all back to me.

Spence, who?

TWENTY-SEVEN
Paul

"Are you sure you're going to be okay?"

Nicole looks around the small room, hands shoved in her back pockets, before looking back at me. "I promise I'll be fine, Paul. It's exactly the right size for just me and fits right in my budget."

I chuckle at her joke. "Yeah, that *zero* on the rent line of your budget looked pretty good."

"And really," she continues, "I have the best landlord. He'll be here every day. I'm sure if there are any maintenance problems, he'll take care of them."

I roll my eyes at her continued use of the word "he" when I'm standing right here.

Over the last few months, I've gotten to know Nicole pretty well. Physically, she's all healed up and you would never know by looking at her that she had such a significant trauma at the hands of someone she loved. Emotionally, that's a different story. She still struggles with nightmares and is nervous around new people, especially men, but she's also determined to push through it all and get her life back.

Step one: move into her own place. And since my old place is vacant as of yesterday, it seems like a great option for her.

Handing her the key to my old apartment, I take a second to confirm one last time. "Are you sure? It's not too late to move in with us."

"And share a room with my nephew? No thank you." She snatches the key out of my hand. "Now if you'll please go to work, I have some boxes to unpack." She pushes me toward the door, and I let her. If I dug my heels in, there's no way all five-foot four-inches of her could move me.

"Okay," I say over my shoulder as I go through the doorway into the hall. "But if you need anything we're just in the front and don't forget to set the alarm—"

The door slams in my face, effectively cutting off the conversation.

"I don't hear any beeps!" I yell, eliciting what sounds like a muffled, "Oh for shit's sake." But then I hear the alarm set so I leave her alone.

The closer I get to the front, the louder it gets. It's a packed house tonight already. I shouldn't be surprised. It's a packed house pretty much all the time now. Word of mouth meant all the professional sports teams in the area started coming here and while their seasons overlap a bit, their off seasons don't, thank goodness. We'd probably be over capacity otherwise.

"Who do we have here tonight?" I ask Kiersten as I climb under the counter and head to the back of the bar to help her.

She gestures to a row of tables that have all been pushed together. "The Steer and some of the Slingers showed up about ten minutes ago. Tammy's getting orders, I'm just prepping." She starts tossing ice inside the metal buckets for bottles to go in as needed. "How's Nicole doing back there anyway?"

I snort a laugh as I begin shoving beer bottles in the buckets she already filled. Worst case, we can store them in the cooler for a while. "She kicked me out."

"Good. I've been telling you for months that you're too overbearing with her."

"Kiersten."

"Paul," she says mocking my stern tone.

"She went through a terrible trauma."

"And she's doing well." Kiersten stands up straight so we can see eye to eye. "I know you're nervous about her living on her own."

I grunt and cross my arms. Nervous is an understatement. I don't like the situation at all.

"But even her therapist says this is good for her. And she's right here on the property. She won't even technically be alone overnight except for a few hours. And you upgraded the security system. She's fine. Let her have her independence back."

It's not like I have a choice. Despite my continued attempts to get Nicole to move in with us in our new apartment, she resisted. These Willoughby women are more stubborn than I give them credit for.

Kiersten sidles up to me and wraps her arms around my neck. It's my favorite thing.

"You're not playing fair. You know I love it when you hold me like this."

She chuckles lightly. "Yes, I do. I also know my sister is going to be fine. She's ready. And she needs this."

I drop a light kiss to Kiersten's lips and pat her backside just because I can. "I don't like it, but I'll try to let it go."

"Think of it this way," she kisses me again. "Now that she's out of my house and Carson has his own room, we don't have to sneak around anymore."

Her comment completely derails any reservations I have. For the last six months, we've gotten closer. All of us. I've bonded with Carson, who I love more than I can even describe, I've gotten close with Nicole who is like a little sister to me, and most importantly, Kiersten and I are madly, sweetly, sickeningly in love. I can't remember what life was like before she came along.

I also can't remember what it was like to try and have sex quietly so a toddler doesn't wake up, or quickly so she can get home at a decent hour. Overnights have been few and far between. The thought of having a bed we share every single night where we can take our time and be as loud as we want?

"Well, I suppose Nicole will be fine on her own."

Kiersten laughs against my lips before giving me a quick peck and getting back to work.

"Listen you two," Tammy demands as she drops her tray on the counter, her signature move whenever she has something she needs to say. "I'm just as excited as you are that you finally moved in together…"

"I highly doubt that," I mutter making Kiersten laugh.

"… but I need you to focus long enough to serve up some booze. I need three buckets of Shiner, two tap IPAs, a margarita on the rocks, and something called a Sazerac?"

"Heath's here already?" I'm surprised he's not home resting from helping Kiersten move again. Poor guy always seems to get suckered into doing all the heavy lifting around here.

"How did you know that was for Heath?" Tammy asks.

"He's the only one who drinks it. I keep trying to push it but he's the only taker."

"Whatever," Tammy says with a wave of her hand. "As long as they're tipping, I don't care what they drink."

She talks a good game, but we all know Tammy absolutely loves the guys. And they love her right back.

"Don't charge Heath anything tonight."

Tammy looks puzzled so I clarify.

"He worked for pizza and booze again. Time for me to pay up."

She lifts her chin, acknowledging how much Heath deserves a few free drinks for all his help.

The three of us make quick work of gathering all the drinks and two of my favorite ladies set off to deliver while I hang back and clean up the mess we've already made. It gives me a few seconds to take in the scene around me and just enjoy.

A year ago, I had just bought this business and it was on the verge of falling apart. Now, we have regular customers who cover more than just the bills every night, a party time studio that gives the best dance teacher I know a financial cushion, a house mascot who never seems to leave the pool table, and I've got the woman of my dreams and the best child I could ask for living with me.

I never saw any of this coming, but I have to admit, if somehow it all falls apart, it won't be because I didn't put in my all. When it boils down to it, that's all any of us can ever do.

Well, that and serve up some damn good drinks.

As Tammy and Kiersten make their way back toward me, I get right back to work, the place where it all finally fell into place.

I look at them both and smile. "Who's next?"

TWENTY-EIGHT

Nicole

"**Y**ou were flirting with him! I saw you!" He grabs my arm and begins squeezing, the strength of his fingertips cutting into my skin. My heart races as I plead.

"No! He asked me where the bathroom was. I was just answering his question!"

His face contorts, his eyes darkening. He looks like pure evil.. "So you could go with him and blow him? Huh? Answer me! Do you want his dick in your mouth?"

"No!" I yell, but he's not listening, too enraged to calm down. "It's you I love! You!"

"You're mine, do you understand? Mine!"

My cheekbone feels like it explodes as he backhands my face. I have no doubt my skin has broken open. The blood is already oozing down my face.

"How dare you make me hit you like this. This is all your fault!"

He roars with anger and... I startle awake, my face pressing so hard into the pillow that my cheek aches.

I quickly run my hand down my face, ensuring there's no blood and it was just a nightmare. It wasn't real, only a nightmare.

Finally satisfied I'm safe in my apartment, I roll onto my back and breathe in… two, three, four, hold… two, three, four, and out… two, three, four. My heart begins to calm and the normal sounds around me start to register.

Another roar from outside my door and I finally put together what woke me up.

Trivia Night at Frui Vita.

Grabbing the remote, I turn the television off and slide my jeans on. I'm not sure how I fell asleep on the couch. I usually don't go to bed until the bar is closed. I must be extra tired tonight. The last thing I remember is someone named Alex being added to *The Circle*. I don't stay awake long enough to find out if he's a catfish.

This is what my life has come to. Living in a small apartment in the back of my almost brother-in-law's bar and binge-watching reality television every night. Pathetic. At some point I need to look at moving on with my life. It's been months since I left my jerk boyfriend, Jeremy. While he still plagues me in nightmares, I want to have a life when I'm awake, not be stuck in this limbo I've found myself in.

Making sure I have my keys, I head out the door locking it behind me, not even caring that my make up probably looks worn from the day and my hair is piled on top of my head. It's late and I doubt I know any of the customers tonight. Heath and his football team are away at training camp and those are most of the guys I know. And only because Heath is my nephew's godfather so he's always around.

I ease my way up to the bar and sit on the stool that I

claimed months ago. I've got my back to a wall, my side to the counter, and I can see every inch of the large room. I feel safest sitting here. I'm also out of the way while my sister works.

Somehow, though she always knows when I join her. I don't even say hello before she's setting a glass of Sprite down in front of me.

"Thanks." I lean on the bar and take a sip of my non-alcoholic beverage, observing the team play happening near the stage. "How's Trivia Night going?"

Kiersten wipes her hands on a towel and grabs the shaker. I'm always in awe watching her work. She's only been here a little over a year and has multi-tasking down pat. "Busy as always."

"Which team is that?" I ask with a gesture of my head. I barely get the question out before more cheers erupt and a huge guy with floppy blond hair stands up so quickly his chair falls backwards. He raises his hands in victory, team-mates holding their drinks up to give him their salud.

My sister just shakes her head with a smirk. "That would be the Slingers hockey team. Kade said they start preseason in a couple weeks. I guess tonight is one last hurrah before hitting the ice hard for the next few months."

"Kade? Is he here tonight?" I pray my cheeks aren't turning pink just from saying his name. Too many people are in my business now as it is. I don't want to tip them off that I may have developed a small crush on him.

It's not even a realistic crush. More like a fantasy of who he might be. If I've learned anything in the last couple of years, it's that fantasy and reality are never the same. Not ever. While I can indulge in a little unrequited interest from afar, I'm not dumb enough to pretend the Kade in my head is the true Kade. I'll never make that mistake with any man again.

Matter of Time is coming December 2021.

237

Acknowledgments

I've just got a few people to thank:

Sometimes a book is just a breath of fresh air to write. This one was like that. Kiersten and Paul's story, while filled with its own issues, was just what I needed so many months into pandemic living. For that, I'm so grateful to them. They may be fictional characters, but Kiersten and Paul became more like family to me and I'm looking forward to meeting with them again.

That doesn't mean they didn't require some work, which leads to the next people I'm grateful for.

Huge shout out to **Brenda Rothert** for talking through ideas with me. The story has so much more depth because of her. And let's not forget how much she advises me on tricks of the trade. You are such a treasure to me!

Andrea Johnston, Hazel James and **Marisol Scott** for the great feedback on this book. I couldn't have done it without you. From the good to the bad and the ugly, I know it ended up all the better because of those giant slashy red pens.

I accidentally forgot to send **McKinnze Lopez** the first draft, which turned out to be a good thing. Knowing how far this book had come and getting your feedback to make it that much better was so important to me. Still aiming for 5 stars, baby!

Let's not forget **Murphy Rae** who created this cover a million years ago and then had to go back and do more with it once it was ready for paperback! Much, much appreciated.

Janice Owen and I have only worked together a handful of times but wow, are you thorough! I'm sorry about the em dashes. If you could tell me where to find them on my computer that would be great, thanks.

My deepest apologies to **Alyssa Garcia** for having to work with me still. You can't get rid of me now!!! (I'm the reason she drinks. Kthanksbye)

Oh and thanks **Mom** for being a last set of eyes. Even when you're wrong, you're usually right. Go figure.

Carter's Cheerleaders, Nerdy Little Book Herd – **you make my world go round!**

Thank you **God** for giving me the words so easily on this one. You promised rest for the weary and you delivered in a big way.

Other books by M.E. Carter

Hart Series
Change of Heart
Hart to Heart
Matters of the Hart
Matters to Me
Matters to You
Matter of Time

Texas Mutiny Series
Juked
Groupie
Goalie
Megged
Deflected

#MyNewLife Series
Getting a Grip
Balance Check
Pride & Joie
Amazing Grayson

Charitable Endeavors
(Collaborations with Andrea Johnston)
Switch Stance
Ear Candy
Model Behavior
Better than the Book

Smartypants Romance
Weight Expectations
Cutie and the Beast
Weights of Wrath